SET IN STONE

* An Elmdale Romance *

LYNN CAMDEN

www.lynncamden.com

Cover design & art by Abra West

Formatting by Jack Harbon

IBSN 978-1-7777577-0-0

For the HBs. The reason this book exists.

For the man who makes me margaritas. It's always you.

Content Notes

Cancer (historic, off-page), death of a parent (historic, off-page), descriptive sex scenes, and anxiety.

"Her heart was a secret garden and the walls were very high."

— WILLIAM GOLDMAN, *THE PRINCESS BRIDE*

SET IN STONE

Chapter One

❧

"Why did I fall for the clickbait raincoat without a hood?"

Grace laughed at the exasperation in my voice. She of course had a perfectly sensible jacket with a deep hood protecting her twist out from the downpour. I had checked the forecast twice throughout the day, but I was still adjusting to how fast the weather on the prairies could turn around. My umbrella was sitting uselessly in my bedroom closet.

"We're almost there, Evie. It's just around the corner." Her tone was patient. A little too patient. "At least your coat is cute and does killer things for your curves. Mine is like a big sack."

It was true, my navy raincoat *was* adorable, with a tiny polka dot pattern and a trench cut that nipped in and flared out over my hips, giving me a more defined waist. It was so rare to find cute plus-sized clothes that I'd entered my credit card information almost on autopilot, hypnotized by the polka dots and the detailing on the pockets. Unfortunately, no one would notice those details because they'd get stuck on how my hair was plastered to my head and how my makeup was running down my face.

"I can't believe I'm going to meet all your friends looking like a drowned rat," I grumbled, raising my voice to be heard over the splashing rain and our hurried steps. Grace waved me off like it wouldn't matter. She and Joel, our other coworker, had been inviting me to go out with their friends for the past four months. I had a feeling she wasn't going to hear any complaints about joining them tonight.

"If you'd come out with us in the summer when it was beautiful out, we wouldn't be having this conversation. Who waits till September to hang out?" Her tone was mild, but I knew I'd been right—she was done with my excuses.

We turned the corner, and I spotted the pub with a stylized lion on the shingle straight away, a warm glow spilling out invitingly from the front windows. It would be the most welcome sight for a chilly, rainy night, if it hadn't been spouting water like a Las Vegas fountain right in front of the door.

"My god, we're going to get swept away before we even get inside."

Grace and I both slowed, intimidated by the waterfall. There must have been a blocked eave-strough creating the solid sheet of icy water in our path.

"We're not getting any drier standing here," I pointed out.

"Right. Run for it?" Grace started her dash almost as soon as she spoke, leaving me in her wake. Her hood saved her, but icy rainwater poured into my collar, soaking the whole back of my shirt. I shrieked as we tumbled inside together, laughing and gasping.

"Remind me to bring an umbrella everywhere I go." I was still breathless.

"And a hood. And a car. In fact, let's just avoid the outdoors altogether," Grace suggested.

A few steps up brought us to the greeter's stand where a server waited for us to collect ourselves. She of course was dry, and perky, with bright berry lipstick and dark dramatic eyeliner that looked fantastic with her light brown skin and made me feel that much more bedraggled.

"Good evening!" She started to ask me if I wanted a table for two but smiled when she recognized Grace, who had just unzipped her coat and taken off her hood. "Oh, hey! Everyone's here already. You can go straight back." She gave me a bigger, more genuine smile now that I had been identified as Grace's friend. The perks of being a regular. From Grace's stories, the Lionshead was like that—a sitcom bar come to life.

I smiled back, hiding my nerves. It wasn't her fault that I was out of sorts and sopping wet. I couldn't decide whether I was more nervous or more annoyed at myself for being nervous. But I was doubly annoyed for showing up looking less than my best when meeting new people. I knew better than anyone how a bad first impression could tank your social credit.

"Thanks, Julia!" Grace brushed by to show me the small coatroom where we hung up our coats far from the others in hopes they'd have a chance to dry.

There was a small mirror in the coatroom, and I checked myself out. I was my usual shade of vampire pale, but because of the cold and our brisk walk, I had developed two bright, almost perfectly round spots on each cheek. With my short black bob plastered to my head, I looked like an old-timey doll. And not in a good way. I found a dry tissue somewhere in an inner pocket of my coat and mopped up the worst of my running eye makeup. Short of fully redoing it, that was the best I was going to look tonight.

Grace came to check herself out, and I made

room for her in the mirror. She clucked her tongue, but she was flawless, of course. Her twist out was pristine, and she was all bounce and gleaming deep brown skin, as usual. She patted a few stray droplets off her face and neck, straightened her earrings, and got out her purse to touch up her lipstick.

I looked out at the street from a little stained-glass window while she finished up. The last half of September had roared in like a lion, declaring that fall was in full swing and getting ready for winter. Each night was a little gloomier, a little rainier, and a little colder than the last. There was beauty in it, of course: in the rippling reflections of streetlamps on glassy wet streets, in the furrows the cars plowed through deep puddles, but those pleasures were best enjoyed indoors, with a muted soundtrack made by the patter of the rain on the roof and the wind shaking rain out of the trees.

Grace nudged me, and we headed out into the cozy atmosphere of the pub. The wood paneling and the beer plaques on the walls all shouted of nostalgia for the UK or Ireland, or some combination of the two. They had Guinness on tap, and the specials on the chalkboard above the bar were all Brit-inspired—bangers and mash, steak and kidney pie, curries, and chips with everything. The clack of pool balls came from further back, and the lighting was warm to the point of being yellow. It was homey and comforting, and the music was just on the edge of too loud. At least I wouldn't have to worry too much about awkward silences.

I followed Grace around the corner of the bar and saw all my hopefully-soon-to-be new friends, Joel waving with exaggerated enthusiasm when he saw us. Grace raised both arms and whooped, curls bouncing. I smiled in spite of my nerves. These two had only ever made me feel welcome, from the very first day I stepped into the campus events office. With them to guide me, a new city, a new apartment, and a new job had been much less overwhelming.

I slid into the booth after Grace. She leaned over and hugged Joel, despite having seen him at work just a few hours ago. Joel had changed out of his work-appropriate black clothes into his casual black clothes, a T-shirt draped on his lean frame. He wore black like it was the only color in the world, and his spiky dark hair contrasted with his pallor—his punk roots ran deep. Over the summer, his genuine interest in me had me blossoming like a teenager who'd just found their first BFF. He and Grace had both drawn me out in their own ways, and it was thanks to both of their constant nagging that I was here with my back sticking to the booth instead of home in my cozy apartment. I waved at him, and he grinned back at me like he could see my mild resentment at being out in the world.

Joel's boyfriend Douglas smiled warmly at me. The last time I'd seen him was when he and Joel had helped me get my new couch up my apartment's treacherous outdoor steps; he good-naturedly bossed both Joel and me around as we maneuvered it. I smiled back. Douglas was red-haired and freckled, with eyebrows so pale they almost disappeared. I had never seen such light eyes on a person before; it was hard to tell if they were blue or green, they were so washed-out. His fingers were entwined with Joel's on the table, like they couldn't go even a minute without touching. My chest ached at that.

"Sorry we're late! Evie and I had to battle the wind on our walk over. And the slippery sidewalks and the puddles made us extra slow." Grace smiled around the table.

Douglas let go of Joel's hand and leaned over to shake mine. The circular booth with its huge table made it a stretch. "Nice to see you again, Evelyn." His eyes crinkled in the corners when he smiled.

The kindness I saw there made me blurt out, "You can call me Evie if you want. Most people do."

It was not strictly true. Past coworkers called me Evelyn. Aunt Bea called me whatever snarky pet name suited her at the moment, and I hadn't had enough friends in high school to warrant any nickname I'd particularly cared for. But I'd always imagined the kind of casual intimacy that came with nicknames. I'd been secretly thrilled when Grace and Joel had started shortening my name on our first day of work together, after asking my permission. The shorthand had made me feel instantly included.

"Joel," Douglas said, looking over at his partner while still holding my hand, "Evie is freezing. Her hands are like icicles. We need to get her something warm ASAP." He was already lifting his hand from mine to signal the server as he finished his sentence. "Do you like hot toddies, honey? They warm you up like nothing else."

I gave a grateful nod, and the server came to take the order immediately. That whirlwind over, I looked around at the rest of the table.

Joel waved around at the other two. "Here we have a sampling of friends and partners in crime! This is Lucy Tan and Aaron DeLuca." Lucy gave me a friendly wave, and Aaron and I exchanged a nod. Joel continued, "We sometimes have others that join for our pub nights, but this is the core group. Now, I think we all know what we're ordering, but we can wait for you to decide."

Lucy laughed at that. "Speak for yourself, Joel! I'm starving." She was cute and short with a tousled bleached-blond pixie and a nose piercing that caught the light when she moved.

Oh no. They had already been waiting for us and were ready to order. Grace had her menu open already and came here often enough that she probably had her meal picked out. I caught up my menu and scanned over the three pages blankly. I should have looked up the website earlier and figured out what to have. Starting to feel like I was spiraling with everyone watching me, I glanced over at Joel with a plea in my eyes. "Any recommendations?"

He looked slightly taken aback at the anxious vibe I was putting out, but put on a suggestive eyebrow waggle that always made me laugh. "Darling, have you tried...bangers? They are juicy and delicious."

I saw Aaron shaking his head across the table, and Grace snorted. I rolled my eyes. It wasn't even very good innuendo. But when the server appeared, I went ahead and ordered the bangers and mash.

She had also brought my hot toddy, the glass cup steaming appealingly, and smelling of honey, lemon, and a whole lot of booze. I was thankful for the distraction while she took everyone else's orders. I needed to take a breath and chill. It had been too long since I'd been in any kind of social situation, and I was really out of practice.

Aaron was sitting across from me, studying his

menu intently, right up until the time the server came to take his order. I could have sworn she either didn't write it down or had it written ahead of time, which puzzled me. He was an attractive man, with big shoulders and arms on a thick-framed body. If he'd approached me at a bar at the right moment, when I was just drunk enough, I'd have jumped at the chance to get arms like those around me.

He had close-cropped brown hair, a thick but neatly groomed beard, and lightly tanned white skin. He and our server seemed to know each other well and had a short back-and-forth, his shoulders lifting in a shrug at something she said before he nodded and handed her the menu with a small smile. She gave him a big flirtatious grin back like she found him charming. I turned back to my drink, now cool enough to sip without scorching my throat.

The group chatted merrily as we waited for our food and thankfully didn't expect me to jump in right away. I relaxed bit by bit, sipping my warm drink, letting the alcohol loosen me up.

I flashed back to past coworker drinking nights at my old jobs, full of poorly concealed barbs, insults disguised as jokes, and backstabbing comments made outright as soon as someone left the table for another drink. Tension and wariness stiffened my posture on those nights, stress dulled slowly by rounds of shots, until I could pretend we were having a good time.

This group was different. Tight-knit, with good-natured inside jokes and half-explained stories flying around the table. Tactile too—elbows dug into ribs and shoulders patted comfortingly when a joke hit too close to home. Douglas was a born prankster, mischief lighting his eyes, and a grin always ready. He kept egging Lucy on to get her to tell stories that set the whole table laughing. Lucy's short pixie got progressively wilder from running her hands through it before beginning each anecdote. She had an appealing rasp to her voice, and her delicate features were perfectly set off by her haircut and the precise flick of her black eyeliner.

Aaron was the obvious magistrate, wading in with definitive statements or making rulings in favor of one party or another. Every time there was an argument, all eyes drifted to him, and he would lift those wide shoulders and drop them again before pronouncing judgment, his deep voice lending him an air of authority. His rulings were always accepted, with the winner crowing over the loser. His bearded chin rested in his hand, a smile quirking the side of his mouth and bringing out a deep dimple that mesmerized me every time it made an appearance.

He glanced at me and caught me staring, and his

eyes flashed as they connected with mine. He turned back to Lucy.

"Tell Evie about the time that Joel signed up for a 300-level agronomy class while drunk, thinking it was anthropology." His half-smile broadened when he looked from her back to me, drawing me into the conversation.

"The best part is that I watched him do it!"

Joel pointed and yelled, "Betrayer!" while Lucy cackled and rubbed her hands together like a maniacal gremlin.

"I loved how when I offered to walk you to class on the first day you had no idea why! And then you didn't wonder at all why it was in the Ag building?"

"I didn't know! I thought maybe it was the only space available!" He looked sheepish. "I still can't believe they let me sign up for that class without any of the prerequisites."

Lucy continued. "And when I looked into the classroom, it was all trucker hats. I just about died seeing your little alternative self sitting there."

"Little. That's rich, coming from you." He shook his head. "I thought I was high, reading the syllabus they handed out. And I was right at the front and couldn't leave during the first lecture. I went straight to the office to drop it after."

He took our laughter with good grace. "I think

one of those trucker hat boys was checking me out, though. I got vibes, believe me." He winked at Douglas and got an elbow in the ribs for being cheeky.

I knew that they'd met at Fox University, my new workplace, but I hadn't realized most of them had been in dorm together in their first year or that some of them had rented a house together for the rest of their Fox U days. They spoke fondly of days at the Jubilee House, their touchstone and landing place through all the stresses of course loads and interpersonal strife. Different housemates drifted through, but the main group stayed the same.

I tuned back in to hear Lucy say, "It felt like everybody was dating each other! You couldn't have a house party without someone sticking their tongue down someone else's throat."

"Ew, Lucy." Grace gagged.

"Thankfully, darling," Joel drawled, "our university days are behind us. Not that it's helped your tongue become any more discriminating." Douglas roared while Lucy stuck the tongue in question out at Joel. Aaron shook his head but fought a smile, and Grace clutched her sides beside me.

Lucy, obviously looking to shift the attention away from her, focused on me. "What about you, Evie? What did you major in?"

She'd caught me off guard, but hopefully not enough to be noticeable.

"Oh! I didn't go to university. I started working right out of high school and have just kept at it ever since." I felt hot, but I tried for a casual smile. "I guess I never really saw a reason to do more school, and I'm glad not to have any student loans to worry about now."

Lucy smiled back. "Good for you. Student loans are killer. I'm only halfway through paying mine off." I nodded back in what I hoped was understanding, but I was desperate for the conversation to turn back to focus on someone else.

It wasn't meant to be. Aaron turned to me again. "And how do you like working at Fox U? Joel mentioned that you aren't from Elmdale. Are you adjusting to life here okay?" He looked like he was ready to take notes on my answer, his brow furrowed and both arms on the table, leaning closer to hear me.

"Yeah, it's been fine." I was taken aback, but the whole table was looking at me, expecting more. "I actually used to live here when I was young, so it's not completely new. I like my little place, and it's within walking distance of Fox U." They were still waiting for more, and the alcohol had warmed me up enough that I kept going. "It's only twenty minutes to walk, and the landlady lives downstairs. She's nice.

And there's a corner store at the end of the block that stocks good fruit and veggies. People so far have been really friendly. From my experience, bigger cities are colder. Everyone is in a rush there."

"Honey, there's no place colder than the prairies." Grace smiled at me. "But I know what you mean. There isn't the same level of pressure here."

Aaron nodded and opened his mouth like he was going to ask me something else, but thankfully, the food came. The server juggled our heavy plates with professional ease, and we all tucked in. My sausages were to die for—fat and juicy, with crispy skin that burst when I cut into them, the juice running out to join the gravy that had been poured generously over a fluffy mound of mashed potatoes. I sighed at the sheer perfection and set to it.

My next few minutes were spent crafting my perfect bites—potatoes and gravy smeared with peas and then stabbed into a round of sausage, each bite a perfect savory package. I paused with a bite ready on my fork, and when I looked up, I was surprised to find Aaron studying me, following my fork's movements. He quickly looked back down at his plate, his shepherd's pie half gone already.

I shrugged and went back to my perfect bite, humming while I chewed. The sausage was lightly flavored with sage and deeply savory and reminded me of Granny. She would have loved the Brit-inspired flavors. She had emigrated in her mid-twenties with two tiny daughters. She was too pragmatic to look back, but she'd kept her cultural touchstones— accent, food, tea snobbery, and a special obsession with British chocolate. Back before there were many international goods stores around, Mum and Aunt Bea would ship Cadbury bars from the UK for her birthday when they could scrape enough cash together for the fees.

Tuning back in to the conversation, I heard Grace and Douglas talking accounting software. He was an accountant too, and she was getting frustrated with the program the university was using. Joel looked resigned to be stuck in the middle of a finance conversation.

I could catch pieces of Lucy and Aaron's conversation, which also sounded like work talk.

"...but of course they won't return my emails now that I'm asking for payment," I heard Lucy say, waving her fork in frustration, a piece of butter chicken nearly sliding off the end.

Aaron looked intent on her problem. His own plate was completely wiped clean, and I wondered if he'd tasted any of it. "Lucy, when we set up your freelance gig, I told you to have a clause in your contract for late payments, remember?"

Lucy rescued the bite of chicken and chewed it while she talked, practically vibrating. "I know, I know! There was just too much to set up, and I didn't get around to it."

"I tried to give you my system for collecting outstanding payments. I'll send you my contract again, and you'll see I've clearly outlined what happens if they miss the payment deadline, including late fees. You can use it as a template." He seemed to soften as she groaned in frustration, and continued in a gentler tone I strained to hear. "I told you contract work was going to be rough if you didn't have these systems in place." The words weren't any less scolding, but he somehow made it sound encouraging rather than nagging.

"You and your systems and your five-point plans. I was hoping you'd pat my head and tell me my clients suck so we could just abuse them for a while." Lucy was whining now, and I hid my smile as I listened in. I'd been in her shoes exactly, wanting sympathy from Aunt Bea but getting sensible advice instead.

"I'll rag on them *after* you email them back with your reminder and threaten them with late fees. Bcc me on the email, and your shots will be on me next week." He raised his nearly empty pint to clink her glass.

I looked over at Joel again, and he rolled his eyes

dramatically for my benefit, bombarded on all sides by money talk. I smiled back and finished my last bite.

It struck me that maybe this was the real advantage I'd missed out on by skipping higher education —I'd never experienced the warmth I felt from how these friends cared for each other and helped each other long after their university days. All my friends in the past decade had been passing work acquaintances, transient as we drifted from job to job, more interested in our own career advancement than helping each other. I couldn't think of a single person in one of my many past jobs that I could call up for advice on how to write a contract.

Douglas stretched his arms overhead and looked around at us as if gauging whether we were done with dinner. He was obviously the one who organized the group's social calendar. He was pretty ripped for an accountant. I caught Joel ogling him and smiled to myself.

Joel really had gone above and beyond for a new coworker. On my very first day, he'd given me his cell and told me to text him when I inevitably got lost on the sprawling campus or in the underground tunnels used in the icy depths of winter. I had texted him 'HELP' approximately thirty times in that first week.

Both he and Grace had been a lifeline in the first

few months of my move, volunteering to help with all the logistics involved in setting up my new place. I had made my space as cozy as I could, and had gone full hermit mode once it was ready. Now, when I got home from work, I changed straight into pj's and made a cup of tea, four-liter and settled in for dinner and as much mindless TV as my eyes could take.

I was thankful that Joel and Grace had been so patient with me and accepted all my excuses about not joining them for an outing with their friends. Joel would just give me his sweet smile and say, "When you're ready." Grace always shook her head, but fondly enough that I didn't feel shamed for turning them down. They knew I wasn't rejecting them; I was just at capacity. But I knew I needed to make the effort now. Socializing was like a muscle, and mine was in danger of atrophying.

"Who's up for a round?" Douglas asked the table, after the server had brought takeout containers for our leftovers.

I must have looked uncertain, because Aaron cleared his throat, and when I looked over at him, he said, "Pool." He had a spark in that intense gaze and a tiny quirk in the corner of his mouth.

Aaron looked at Douglas and tilted his chin in challenge, flashing him a smirk, smug and compelling. I found myself eyeing him again appreciatively. "You think you can bring something better than usual, Thompson? Should I spot you a few balls this time?" His tone was a flag fluttering in front of a bull.

I looked around the table. Everyone was grinning, the light of competition already shining from their faces, transforming them in a split second, making me suddenly uneasy. Was this where the fault lines in this group of friends would finally show?

Chapter Two

❧

"Now, Evie, you"—Douglas pointed at me with his cue, firmly in command—"will break."

"Will I?" Everyone laughed my deer-in-the-headlights expression. Suddenly I couldn't remember how to breathe. Was it normal to hold on the inhale? *Friends. These are friends. Take a breath.* I went through my routine as discreetly as possible: dropping my shoulders, unclenching my hands, emptying my lungs on a slow count of four before pausing and starting the four-count again on the inhale. I could almost feel Aunt Bea's hand on my shoulder, coaching me through each breath. *Okay. I was okay.*

Pool had turned out to be a serious proposition. Once we'd headed over to the pool tables and our server had hooked us up with a rack, I realized that there must have been some extracurriculars I'd missed out on in those university years too. Everyone expertly picked their favorite cue and chalked up, and I had been left standing to one side at a loss.

Douglas kept chalking his cue thoroughly, not noticing my turmoil. *There's no spotlight on you. Everyone is thinking about themselves.* "It's simple, Evie." He grinned at me. "You're going to be on my team, and we are going to beat Aaron and Lucy so thoroughly that they'll never recover."

"No pressure," Joel drawled from the other side of the table.

"That's enough out of you, my love. You'll have your turn next round," Douglas said.

I looked over at Lucy and Aaron. She had turned to chat with Grace, seemingly not as invested in whatever was happening over here. Aaron was watching me and Douglas, eyes hooded, while he slowly chalked his cue. My panic spiked again at his attention, the feeling of a spotlight so bright it blinded me.

Douglas, seeming not to notice my stress, handed me his chalked cue and motioned me to the front of the table. I leaned down and gave it my best effort, feeling so awkward that I thought I might just expire on the spot. I managed enough force to separate three balls off the rack but everything else may as well have been glued to the table.

There was a pause, and then Lucy asked, "What on earth was that?" Her fists were on her hips like I'd let down every woman in history.

"I'm sorry! I've only played a few times, and no one taught me anything! Someone else can break, and I'll go stand in the corner." I managed a laugh, but knew I was red.

Douglas wouldn't hear it. He racked again and made me try again. "Here, line up, try not to hit the head ball straight on but come at it a little from the side. Give it a good strong hit, straight line, as much force as you can without losing control."

I decided that the fastest way to get this very public lesson over with was to try it. My second try was a little better, and Douglas deemed it enough of an improvement that we could carry on with the game. Of course, playing with experienced people meant the balls were all gone long before I was up again.

When they started to rack another game, I begged off. "I'm honestly not adding anything to your game by standing around holding a cue. I'll just sit on one of those stools and watch." I gestured to the back wall behind me with bar stools and high tables.

Grace tried to catch my arm and make sure I was

okay, but I waved her off with a smile. I was happy to sit and watch, recover from that momentary anxiety spike, and get more familiar with the group dynamics. They were an odd number without me, but they seemed used to working around it, rotating out and in seamlessly.

On the next round, Lucy joined me at my table and ordered us both another drink, keeping me entertained with her graphic design horror stories from her previous work and with her new freelance venture. I gasped at the appropriate moments to encourage her to keep talking.

"Freelancing has been way better. I don't have everything ironed out yet, but at least I can control my own schedule. And refuse a client if I don't think we fit." Lucy shrugged and sipped at her pint.

"I overheard you and Aaron talking about contracts before. Sounds rough."

"Really not my favorite part of the job. He's been helping me get all that set up, but it comes with a side of nagging." She rolled her eyes.

"Wait. Are you two together?" The thought was a splash of cold water to the face. They had been chatting with heads together all evening. I didn't know why I didn't see it.

A snort ripped out of her loud enough to startle. "Aaron? Hell no." She tilted her head to the side and lifted a hand in a half shrug, conceding a point. "We did go on a few dates early on. The chemistry was not there. Kissing him was...let's just say I'm not into beards."

Bearded kisses flashed through my head, and I shook the pictures away. Had everyone in this group dated each other? I couldn't imagine dating under a microscope like that. And they had continued as friends after without perishing of awkwardness? I would have turned into a ghost and forged new ID.

Grace bounded up to us to tag Lucy in. She jumped onto the stool across from me still sparking with victory, top and bottom teeth flashing in her exuberant smile as she threw a middle finger Joel's way after sinking the winning ball.

"So, what do you think of the crew? Isn't Douglas great? And Lucy and Aaron too?"

"Yes, they're all great! Lucy has the best stories. And it's nice to get to know Douglas a bit better. He and Joel fit well together." I loved watching them weave in and out of conversation. Not attached at the hip, but always reconnecting over the course of the evening.

"Totally. Any time Joel is off the wall with too many ideas and projects, Douglas helps ground him. They had a rough start, but they've really figured things out now." Grace sighed dreamily. "I'm so happy for them. I can't wait to find something like they have one day."

Grace was the most selfless person I'd ever met. If she said she was happy for one of her friends, she was dancing-up-and-down, cheering-them-on kind of happy.

"Are you actively looking at the moment? Did you download that dating app Melanie was talking about at lunch the other day?" Our admin was young and very cool, and she dated like she had to meet every eligible man in the city in person in order to prevent a nuclear war. She was a woman on a mission. She had kissed a lot of frogs and had the stories to prove it. On the other hand, she was getting way more action than either Grace or me, so apparently all that hustle paid off.

My action consisted of a few excellent vibrators. I was starting to forget what the weight of a man felt like. Maybe I should get a cat.

Grace was shaking her head. "I have way too much stranger danger to get on those apps. Have you never listened to a true-crime podcast? I will end up murdered in an alley somewhere." She shushed my protests that she was perfectly safe. "No. What I need are better friends that can set me up with people they know who aren't serial killers, or married, or men who refuse to get therapy." She paused. "Or all three at once, I suppose."

"Oh, I'm *so sorry* I've been letting you down all these months." I was all sarcasm. "Have I mentioned that I'm new to the city?" She waved me off. "What about one of your Jubilee House friends? Have you never had any sparks within this group?"

She grimaced. "I don't shit where I eat. Can you imagine?" When I shook my head, she continued. "There was so much drama early on with in-house dating and weird breakups that I decided never to go there. And by now, I've seen them all puke from too much partying and just be generally disgusting. They've entered brother status now."

She stared off into space, caught in memories, and refocused on me with obvious effort. One blink later, I could practically see the light bulb over her head turn on. "You!" She pointed dramatically, her dark red nails underscoring the moment.

I gasped with fake astonishment, a hand to my chest. "Me!"

"Shut up," she replied. "You should date Aaron! You guys would be a great match!"

"Absolutely not." I needed to shut this down as emphatically as possible before she got carried away. The gleam of matchmaking shone bright in her eyes, amping up my discomfort. "I'm not into..." I flailed to find an obvious flaw. "Beards. I'm not into them." She didn't need to know this was a blatant lie.

She started to marshal some argument in his favor, but I cut her off. "Aaron is the last person I'd be interested in. Trust me." I talked over her so she wouldn't pester me, but after I blurted it out, Grace practically choked on her last sip of beer, making me realize that that the hot toddy and the Guinness I'd had after it might have impaired my volume controls.

I followed the direction of her gaze and saw Aaron standing nearby, looking at me like he'd heard everything. His brows were down. Oops. If I was red earlier, now my cheeks were so hot my I felt like my face was melting. I could feel the flush crawling down my neck, the angry red blotches all over my throat.

Grace cleared her throat, getting my attention again. Her face was stuck on "yikes."

"It's okay, Evie." She was so quiet I could barely hear her, in marked contrast to my outburst. "He's a great guy. That's all I was going to say. If there's no chemistry, that's cool."

Douglas's call interrupted our awkward moment, and it was her turn to play. I gulped at my ice water, trying to cool down and recover.

Unfortunately for my loud mouth, it was Aaron's turn to sit out. That must have been why he was close enough to overhear me. He had been heading over to tell Grace to spell him off.

He came over like nothing had happened, and I tried a small smile in his direction that he didn't acknowledge. Instead, he waved the server over and ordered another Guinness, raising an eyebrow at me to silently ask if I wanted anything. I shook my head no. I'd definitely had enough.

Having him perched on the stool opposite me made me acutely aware of how small the table was and how much space he took up. I took him in with sidelong glances, pretending interest in the neon signs on the walls. His deep green hoodie was draped loosely over his thick torso. Solid was the word for him. Something that you'd need power tools to budge. When the server returned with his beer, he wrapped one paw around it, resting it on the table. I was unnerved by that hand. It looked like he regularly hammered nails with his fists.

I wondered if he was going to say something, maybe call me out for being rude about him. Though, he really should have tried not to listen to a private conversation between girlfriends. But he didn't say anything. He turned his body away to watch his friends play pool like it was the final inning of game seven of the World Series.

I could admit to being miffed at being so thoroughly ignored. What was he thinking about? Did he care that I wasn't interested in him at all? I tried to tune into the game, but my eyes kept getting drawn back to tracing the path up from his meaty fist, to the round of his shoulder, to the shape of his neat beard.

I got caught on one slow perusal. He'd turned his head and had been watching me on that whole embarrassing journey up his torso. Our eyes connected, and I bounced mine straight back to the pool table, my pulse leaping. Had I imagined that mouth quirking up before I looked away?

I was grateful for the commotion of impending victory to distract myself. Douglas had surrendered the table to Grace, who cleared it handily, raising her fists and whooping over Douglas and Lucy's groans. She and Joel did a chest bump that would have been ridiculous if she'd had my cup size but worked with her lean figure.

I caught sight of the clock above the bar and made my way over to my friends to tell them I had to head out. Joel caught my hand. "Evie, you have to let us drive you home. Douglas will be happy to drop you, and Grace will go with Lucy. You can't walk home at this time of night."

I was glad to agree, though I felt bad making them leave early. Douglas read me correctly and said,

"Don't even worry about it, dear Evelyn. We would have been leaving soon anyway." He glanced over at Grace and added, "And I need to go before I get beat again."

Lucy and I hugged goodbye, and I promised to come again.

I began to make my way back to our coats, but a touch stopped me abruptly. A big hand cupped the point of my elbow, firm but fleeting. I whirled around to find Aaron, both hands now holding out my box of leftovers I'd abandoned at our table like an offering.

"You forgot this," he said simply.

"Thanks." I mustered up a final smile, but I could not think of a single other word to say. "Goodbye," I muttered, too preoccupied with my brain freeze to be any more gracious.

He nodded back, and I fled toward the dim sanctuary of the coatroom.

After Grace and I zipped into our jackets, we stepped out into the cold, wet dark to make the short dash to the car. Joel produced an umbrella like magic from one of his coat pockets, and I took his arm to walk under it with him, thankful for shelter from the steady rain.

Chapter Three

❦

Monday morning Grace and I were
catching up in my office over coffee
when Joel burst in with his phone held
aloft like an Olympic flame.

"Guess who's blowing up my phone asking about
Evie?"

"Who?" I had a bad feeling about this.

Grace looked at me like I'd said something
incredibly dense. She shook her head and turned
back to Joel. "What did he say? And why isn't he
texting me?" They were both ignoring me completely.

Joel scoffed. "This is bro talk. It's not for the likes
of you. We're business bros for life."

Grace threw up her hands in disgust. "Joel, that
makes no sense. I was the one who stuck it out in

business school with him, and you dropped out. If anyone is a business *sis,* it's me. Who helped him pass stats? This is the thanks I get? I should have let that boy fail." She looked ready to march out and give someone a piece of her mind.

"You can't be business sis to him," Joel scoffed again. "It sounds wrong. There are too many 's' sounds. It's a kids' book run amok. There'll be a cartoon snake next." He waved his phone around for emphasis, still lit up and open to his texts.

Grace was gearing up for another round, but this was getting out of hand. I wanted both of them out of my office.

I cleared my throat pointedly, and their eyes swung toward me, breaking their staring competition. "Hi. Yes, I'm still here!" I waved. "We've gotten off track. Who is texting and why? I have a few minutes, and then I need to head out for my meeting with the School of Social Work." I looked down at my notes and frowned. "Grace, if you have a minute, can you help me check over their budget? Because I think it's wildly unrealistic for the size of event they want."

"Stop changing the subject!" Joel burst out.

"Start talking, and I won't have to."

Joel grabbed the other chair from the corner where it had been tucked out of the way and got comfortable. I didn't much like the look of his posture, with his long legs stretched out in front of him, casually crossed at the ankle, sport coat unbuttoned. He looked like he was settling in for a week, and my to-do list today was too long for that. I glanced pointedly at my watch and back at him.

"Aaron. You've made an impression." He pursed his lips thoughtfully, assessing my reaction.

I kept my face as neutral as possible. Grace nodded placidly, not at all surprised. She too had crossed her long, elegant legs, slim and flexible enough to have the top foot almost touch the ground. I felt the smallest twinge of thigh envy before checking myself.

Joel was still looking at me expectantly. I wasn't sure what he wanted from me, but my heart sank when I remembered how rude I'd been that night.

"I'm sorry, okay?" I looked down and started twisting my ring, too embarrassed to meet either of their eyes. The emerald green that was my shared birthstone with Mum circumnavigated my finger, giving me a pang every time it came around to the front. "I didn't mean for him to hear that. I guess that second drink was a bad idea, and I blurted it out without thinking. I shouldn't have said it. I know he's your friend, and it was rude of me."

I looked up at last. Joel was staring at me open-mouthed, eyes flicking back and forth like he was trying to solve a math problem. Grace had a hand over her mouth, her head turned to the side. Was she upset about it too? She had seemed fine earlier. Joel decided that I was no longer worthy of conversation and turned to Grace.

"What the hell is she talking about?"

Grace let out a snort. Her shoulders were shaking with what I finally realized was repressed laughter. She shook her head and started digging in the bag at her side, still vibrating silently. She came up with a tissue and dabbed at her eyes.

"You missed it, Joel," she said, finally winding down enough to talk. "Poor Evie here basically yelled that she wouldn't date Aaron if he was the last man on earth. Pretty sure our boy heard that one."

I couldn't help another internal cringe at the memory of him sitting down next to me afterward. Was his silence a reproof, or did he not care? The thought of his eyes connecting with mine, of him watching me check him out sent hot shame down my spine. Moving away was my only option. Antarctica was probably beautiful this time of year.

Comprehension and humor lit Joel's face. He shrugged back with a smirk that I wanted to wipe right off.

"Evie, Evie," he said in an infuriatingly chiding tone. "You've done it now."

"Yeah," Grace agreed. "Talk about waving a red flag in front of one very stubborn bull."

Joel nodded and talked right over my feeble attempt to interject. He was still turned toward Grace, making me feel like I wasn't even in the room. "He's never backed down from a challenge. Ever. Remember the time I bet him he couldn't drink a four-litre of milk?"

"That was gross. Why do you remind me of all the gross things I've had to endure in your company? Why do I hang out with so many boys?" Grace threw up her hands. "I can't believe you would bring up the milk and not, like, how he got his business degree and then did three years of apprenticeship after? Are we fifteen?"

She turned to me, still outraged. "Evie, kick this man out of your office. I am done with all his frat boy energy."

"Actually, you both have got to go. I can't deal with either of you right now, *and* I have to leave for my meeting in ten. So shoo."

I sprang up and ushered them out before they could protest, and, catching my chair on its next revolution, I sank back into it. I picked up my coffee and went down my list a final time, grimacing at my next cold sip.

I should have been reviewing the budget that I couldn't make heads or tails of, but my mind wandered back to Aaron. He had been asking about me. I was suddenly annoyed. I'd tamped down any stray attraction to him just to avoid this kind of attention. I had almost succeeded. I'd shut Grace down. And then he had to go and barrel his way into my workday. This is what came of having actual friends. If I'd kept things more casual, I'd have been coasting along in my office by myself with my door closed all morning.

Grace's easy laughter drifted through my open door, pricking my conscience. I wasn't ready to dismiss these new friends. I thought back to all the times they'd helped me already—picking out linens and towels after my first month's pay went through, scouring second-hand shops with me for kitchen essentials, and wrestling furniture up my stairs.

If I was honest with myself, Grace and Joel weren't really overstepping. Even though I'd tried to deny it, Aaron had sparked my interest as much as I had seemingly sparked his. He just seemed so . . . grown-up, even though we were probably the same age.

My meeting reminder dinged and startled me

back to the present. I collected myself, gathered up my folders, and checked my face in my phone before heading out.

The walk to Social Work only took a few minutes. Some of the trees in the courtyard were valiantly holding on to their yellow and orange leaves, but most had been blown bare by all the wind and rain. Winter wasn't far off now.

Grace had taken one look at me in the cute forest-green pea coat I'd bought last year (on sale!) for winter and told me flatly that I'd be wearing it for two months max and to invest in something filled with down. I'd scoured the internet for down jackets in plus sizes that were not also pink camo print—who knew that was a thing?—and thankfully found an option that only cost most of one paycheck. It was on its way to me now, and I checked the tracking on it almost hourly.

The meeting was torturous—not because they weren't lovely people, but because they had no idea how unrealistic their event expectations were. I listened to their enthusiasm and plans and took notes with increasing anxiety over how I would have to disappoint them. They had champagne dreams on a beer budget. When I had four pages of notes on their ideal event plan, I knew I had to cut them off.

"I'll run some more numbers and make some calls.

I'll get back to you by next week Wednesday with a final quote, and then we can discuss how you want to proceed." I gathered my files with an air of finality and made my escape before the dean could think of something else to add.

I sighed as soon as I closed the door behind me, slumping my shoulders forward and tilting my head back and forth to relieve the tension I'd built during the meeting.

I pulled out my phone to text Joel and let him know I was bringing back lattes from the cafe in the University Center before heading back to the office.

The forty-five new messages notification had me blinking in surprise. There was a brand-new group thread sitting in my texts. Gaping, I swiped into them and scrolled back up. Joel had added me to a group chat called "Pub Nights." I scanned all of the texts, noting three different unknown numbers that probably belonged to Lucy, Aaron, and Douglas. The thread would have to go on mute until I had fortifications. New group chats required carbs and caffeine.

Waiting in the long, snaking line for coffee, I called Aunt Bea, judging that she'd be on her lunch hour. Hearing her voice in my ear was steadying, grounding, even as she flitted lightly from topic to topic and lifted my spirits along the way. After hearing about the students she was helping, which coworkers would not stop battling over the thermostat, and what she'd seen while walking Daisy that morning, she turned her attention to me.

"You should get a dog! You love to walk, and I hate thinking of you all alone."

"I'm used to it, Aunt Bea. And I'm happy with my place as it is. Honestly, it's still weird to me that you have Daisy. Mum hated indoor animals."

"Well, Dot can go ahead and spin in her grave, because I adore having a pup to fuss over. I'm sure you would enjoy it too." The note of defiance in Aunt Bea's voice made me smile. Mum had ruled in our household after we'd all moved back in together to take care of Granny. When she had to work overtime at the grocery store, she would call to make sure we were finishing the chores and hadn't burned down the apartment. Even after she got sick, she found the energy to keep the two of us in line.

"My place is too small for a dog anyway. I did consider getting a cat the other day." I didn't mention that it was because I was touch-starved. Some things you just didn't talk about while in a coffee line surrounded by students, even if they were all chatting or texting and ignoring me completely. "Plus, with the amount of moving I do, it's not exactly fair to an animal to drag them through all that chaos."

"Animals are very resilient, you know. Cats can make good moving companions. I saw a charming video of a young man who travels by bicycle from place to place and takes his cat along. Every week they're in a new town together. It was very sweet." Aunt Bea was obsessed with video compilations about pets on social media.

"It takes all kinds, I guess. But even I'm not that nomadic."

"I was hoping you'd put your wandering ways behind you for a while, now that you've made such good friends in Elmdale."

I interrupted that line of conversation before she could get any further with it. "I have to go, Aunt Bea, I'm next up. Call you later?"

She signed off in her usual way, making me smile at the thought of her coworkers seeing her in her office on the phone at lunch and wondering who she was dramatically blowing kisses at.

Juggling a tray of lattes and a bag of muffins while wrangling my scarf in the wind was nearly impossible, but thankfully Melanie was there to take the tray off my hands as I came in. I smoothed my short bob back down and hung my coat before snagging two lattes and a muffin and strolling into Joel's office and plopping all of it down on his desk.

"You gotta help me with this one," I said,

rummaging through my big shoulder bag for my notes.

"That bad, hey?" He picked up his latte and lifted it toward me in a silent cheers before taking a sip.

I broke apart the giant muffin and put half on a napkin for him. We were having his favorite today, which meant chocolate with chocolate chip. My favorite was the blueberry with the crunchy brown sugar topping, but I was the supplicant here.

"I think their eyes are too big for their budgets, so to speak. They want College of Medicine Gala on a church-basement-dessert-fundraiser budget." I paused to take a sip of my latte and sighed. "They're talking about bringing in student volunteers. They also want to do it in a month. The timeline is ridiculous. To add insult to injury, they've already been promoting it to donors but didn't think to contact us. Dr. Gossman also apparently made a verbal agreement to book Rice Hall." I was waving my latte around wildly now. "She expects miracles but isn't working with me at all! Verbal agreement! BAH."

"Let it out, Evie, let it out." He waited while I set my latte down and shook out my hands, relieving some of the pent-up anxiety. "I think we can make something work. It might not be as grand as they would like, but it can be a stepping stone for next year. And the students will be fine. If anyone can wrangle them, it's you. Most of them probably have server jobs anyway." He nudged my muffin half closer to me, encouraging me to take a bite. "How much do we need to cut, and where can we take it from?"

I paused with my muffin in hand. "We need to knock it down to a third. The biggest chunk is catering. I'm not sure how to make that one work."

Joel nodded and turned to his computer, bringing up his contacts. "I have a connection at the culinary school. They might do it near cost for us."

That got me thinking. "I could work with that. We could pull together enough table decor with what we have in storage too."

Joel nodded and pulled up the floor plan for Rice Hall. "Now, how many did you say she wanted to seat?"

We worked away at the event plan, and by the time lunch rolled around I was feeling better about it. Once I got all the quotes I needed and confirmed that the hall was booked, I would breathe easier. When I got up to leave, Joel stopped me at the door.

"Gear up your kick-ass professional voice. You're going to need it." He grinned. "Gossman is a tough nut to crack, but I have confidence in you."

It was good that someone did. I was about to beam back at him when I remembered what he had done.

43

"By the way. Group thread, Joel? Really?"

He spread his hands wide, the furthest thing from repentant. "You were a hit. Lucy already asked when we'd see you again. Douglas demanded to know why you hadn't joined us earlier. And Aaron..." He shrugged. "You made an impression. Adding you to the group thread seemed easier than being your secretary and taking messages for you."

I narrowed my eyes. He had stopped short of telling me the kind of impression I'd made. He certainly hadn't been so coy earlier.

"Joel." My voice was syrupy sweet. "Next time, ask first. Or don't be surprised when your number is blocked." The goddess of directness must have overtaken my spirit. I could think back to a dozen scenarios like this in the past where I would have held my tongue and seethed inside. Maybe someone else would consider this a weak set-down, but I felt light, buoyed by my newfound boldness.

Joel got up and moved in front of me. He sure looked repentant now. "I'm sorry, Evie. Douglas is right. I can be impulsive. I'll remove you right away. I should have checked with you." He held out his hands. "I'm sorry."

I took his hand in my free one and squeezed it once. "Okay. Thanks for apologizing. I'll stay in the chat for now."

It struck me as I returned to my office that I never doubted that he could take my honesty. I should have felt the rising surge of anxiety in my chest, but all I felt was satisfied. My lunch hour was open. With a spark of curiosity burning bright, I swiped my phone open, ready to take on the group chat.

Chapter Four

The rest of the week passed in a blur, the final logistics for the English department's fall alumni fundraiser and mixer taking up most of my time. Thankfully, I didn't have to attend because the admin staff was hosting the event. All I had to do was keep my ringer on high all weekend, just in case there were any questions.

I had wanted to slink home on Friday and stay in bed all weekend, but I had promised the group chat I would be more regular at the pub, so on Saturday night I broke out of my cocoon and walked over. Thankfully it wasn't raining, just cold with a wet fog that helped the chill penetrate every layer. My fabulous but impractical rain jacket had been benched in favor of my green pea coat, and it was doing its best to keep me warm.

When I got in, I saw my friends gathered around the pool tables. I'd been told tonight would be about pool, beer, and snacks. I was not so much into the pool, but the snacks and the company called to me.

Someone came in behind me as I was arranging my coat on the hanger and reached for the coat hanger beside mine. I looked up over my head and saw a big hand and a thick wrist, exposed by the sweater creeping down his arm. I turned my head away and caught a glimpse of Aaron's reflection in the small mirror opposite as the subtle scent of citrus crept around me. I edged a little further away and busied myself fussing over straightening the shoulders of my coat over the hanger, draping my scarf just so over top.

"Hey." Aaron's voice was too close behind me.

I turned, nearly spinning right into him, catching myself at the last minute. His reflexes were faster, and he grabbed my arm to steady me. A minute shiver emanated from that small point of contact before I suppressed it. His hand was warm and firm and cupped around the point of my elbow again. Elbows should not be an erogenous zone.

I shifted back, and his hand instantly dropped. *He's been asking about me.* I forced myself to take my gaze up past his beard and look in his eyes. The light was low enough to make the moment feel intimate.

His gaze was guarded, long dark lashes prominent, and thick eyebrows drawn. His short dark hair looked damp. I realized suddenly that I was staring, and quickly dredged up a smile, belatedly trying for cool and casual.

"Oh, hi! How are you?" Too squeaky and breathless. I cleared my throat subtly and added more warmth to my voice. "How was your week, I mean?" I had to stop there. The group chat had not enlightened me on what he did for work. My small talk needed more practice.

He nodded at me like nothing had happened, "Fine thanks. Finished a big job this morning, and I'm taking tomorrow off." He said it matter-of-factly, like I should know exactly what the job was, how long he'd been doing it, and even what he did at it.

I felt weird asking him anything further so I mustered up an answering smile, backing away from him all the while. "Great! Well, I hope it's a good day off."

I took another half step out of the coatroom and looked around exaggeratedly. "Oh, I think Grace is looking for me. I'm going to go check in with her." I trilled a little false laugh at the end and wished for merciful death, but he just followed my lead and headed over with me, an awkward half step behind me, almost like we were walking in together, but with plausible deniability. Like he was walking a step behind the Queen.

Would I ever come to a night at the Lionshead Pub and not have a nervous flush through most of it? Was I so unaccustomed to company that I couldn't handle it anymore?

I flashed back to the last night out I'd had at my old job. Kirsten—never call her Kristen—had sneered about all of our coworkers in turn as soon as they left the table, and I hadn't missed her pointed remark that Angelica was gaining weight, made to me, the only plus-sized person in our department. That night I'd gotten so drunk the room spun and hit on a dental hygienist just to extricate myself from my miserable coworkers. His face was perfectly unremarkable, his blindingly white teeth the only thing I remembered about him.

Looking back to that time, I hardly recognized myself. When I compared those hectic, resentful, guarded days with the new life I had on the prairies, I wondered why I had let myself be so miserable for so long.

I found Grace and Lucy with their heads together, giggling over something, and felt relief spread through my whole system. My shoulders finally dropped from their tense position around my ears.

"Hi! I'm so glad to see you. I am done with this week."

Grace hugged me, and I was pleasantly surprised when Lucy got up and did too.

"Did you come in with Aaron? What was so hellish about your week? What's that shade of lipstick?"

I laughed at Lucy's rapid-fire questions. "Should I answer them in order? No, everything, and berry bliss."

Lucy looked not at all satisfied, but Grace cut her off saying, "No, no, food and drinks first. Then interrogation."

We ordered what I judged to be most of the appetizer menu before settling in with our drinks of choice. I opted for the house white, and I was keeping it to one this time.

The guys were all standing around the pool table, catching up. I liked them, but it was more comfortable to ease into the evening with Grace and Lucy.

We could not be a more opposite trio—Grace with her long lean limbs elegantly arranged, her hair in knots tonight. She had done her eyes in a dramatic cat eye, and her lipstick was so dark blue it was nearly black. She killed.

Lucy was shorter than me, perched on her stool precariously. Her spiky, bleached-blond hair set off her big eyes and wide cheekbones to perfection. When I complimented her, she told me she'd waited until she left for college to cut it, and her mother had cried when she'd seen it.

I had played up my curves for the night, going all out to celebrate the weekend. My black velvet corset top dipped low and mounded my cleavage under the tight long-sleeved shirt I wore underneath. The corset ended at my hips and my shirt flared over the snug leather leggings paying tribute to my ass. Less pirate wench and more goth girl. I'd done my lips in berry and plumped my lashes as high as I could get them. I was not ashamed to admit I was feeling myself.

I told Lucy all about my events clients, complaining about the English department staff and how many calls I'd had to field already. Grace twirled her cocktail pick back and forth between her fingers, waiting for me to wind down. She'd heard all my current work rants before. She cut in before I could ask Lucy about her design projects, motioning us closer together over the round table.

"We need to talk about the good stuff before the men come back here and ruin our fun. As soon as the food comes, they'll be crowding like vultures."

Lucy nodded and leaned in conspiratorially. "Lay it on me. I want details."

We looked incredibly suspect. I lowered my voice to a volume appropriate for an undercover agent. "Okay, I'll go first. I'm thinking of getting a cat."

Grace rolled her eyes and sat back upright. "That's not the pussy you should be thinking about."

Lucy and I both gasped. I leaned across the table to smack Grace's arm. "I can't believe you!"

"It was right there. You can't blame me when you teed it up so perfectly." She took a smug sip of her cocktail. "Aaron is the topic at hand, FYI." She started ticking off points on her long fingers. "One: He's been texting Joel about you. Two: He came in with you, heeling like a well-trained puppy. Three: He's been staring. In fact, he's staring right now." Her smug smile broadened before she pressed her lips together, tamping it back down.

I couldn't help myself. My brain short-circuited, and my neck swiveled all by itself. My eyes connected with Aaron's across the room, drawn to his like opposite poles of a magnet. I felt the click as we connected, before I regained control of my head and swung back to Grace, wide-eyed and flushed again. I felt like thumping my head on the table. What was I doing?

"Shit." That was all that came to mind.

"What?" Grace squinted at me. "He's hardly a troll. He's actually great. Like, calls his mom, runs his business, is a good friend, shows up if his people need him. He's a catch." She paused, tapping a manicured nail on her chin. "Maybe I should go for him."

It was Lucy's turn to smack her arm "Focus, G. Evie, are you seeing someone, or did you have someone back home who broke your heart or something? We don't mean to pressure you."

I had a lump in my throat, and the wine was not dissolving it. I cleared it. "No, there's no one. I..." I cleared my throat more forcefully. "I've never really had what you'd call a relationship."

They both stared back.

"What exactly would you call them?" Grace asked.

I thought about it for a moment, swirling my wine glass on the table. "Acquaintances with benefits? Bar hookups? If Aaron had walked up to me and hit on me and we were both drunk and then we made out on a dance floor, I'd be more in my element. But he seems like a serious kind of dude. Plus he's asking his friends about me, which is too high school for me to cope with." I raised both hands helplessly. "I didn't even do high school *in* high school. I'm not about to start now."

"You didn't go to high school?" Douglas spoke almost in my ear and startled me. I didn't realize he'd come in time to hear that last. A moment later and they were all there, pushing together more tables and shuffling chairs around to make room. Their timing was impeccable because suddenly our server was there too, a tray full of platters and plates for sharing. She took more orders for drinks and wings from the guys before she left.

Douglas parked himself on the stool beside me and swigged the last of his beer. "So, what were you saying about not going to high school?"

"Oh no, I went. I was just so busy I stayed out of the usual high school drama."

"Oh?" Aaron swiped a big pile of nachos from the platter and grinned unrepentantly at Lucy when she squawked, before focusing on me again. "What were you busy with?"

That grin was quite something. I filed it away for later. "Nothing very fun. My mom was sick. She needed help at home, so I fit school in around that." The lump was back, but I spoke around it. "She passed after I graduated."

The table went quiet with murmurs of sympathy, and heads tilted or bowed to give me a moment. But I was done grieving. Nearly ten years had passed since, and I wasn't going to mourn forever. I smiled around, trying to lighten the moment again.

"Thanks, everyone. It was a long time ago. Joel, can you pass the potato skins?"

Conversation started up again as we passed around plates and pattered on in snippets of shared stories and updates on mutual friends. Somewhere along the way I lost track of the chatter and found myself gazing absently across the table at Aaron and Joel, watching them rib each other, tracking Aaron's hands moving as he talked, appreciating the profile his beard and long nose made, counting the number of times a dimple bracketed one side of his face in a lopsided grin. I idly wondered what it would take to earn a full smile and whether he had a dimple on the other side too.

Douglas nudged me, and I tuned back in to Lucy describing the client she turned down in great detail. "NO, I am not designing your hypnosis website!" Grace was killing herself laughing. "He truly wanted me to embed eyes and spirals in scrollwork around the edges. I mean, come on, I have some standards." She snorted. "He wanted some old-school Flash nonsense, but I do not have time to sink the hours into recreating that."

Douglas laughed too and blew a kiss over toward Joel, who caught it and put it in his breast pocket. Cheesy, but cute as hell. He turned back to us. "So, what else is on the gossip menu tonight? Boys? Sex? Drugs? Horrible bosses?"

Grace replied wryly. "Sorry, Dougie, we got

nothing for you. And what do you have for us? We could use some dirt." She made gimme motions with her hands and shimmied her shoulders at him.

He grinned at her, "Well, dearies, Chris has apparently reactivated his dating profile." Grace's smile froze on her face. He didn't seem to notice. He turned to acknowledge Lucy's sounds of surprise. "That's right, our man is back on the market after getting his heart beat into the ground by the harpy."

I glanced at Grace, concerned, before turning back to Douglas. "Who's Chris? And what happened to him?"

"Chris is another friend from business school. He's not around much at the pub because his kid is young. We sometimes go to his place to hang out so he can put Rosie to bed."

Lucy shook her head. "My god, the harpy fucked him up bad. Like, used and abused. And we all stood around and watched because he would not hear a word against her. So we had to wait until she eventually dropped him and then help him pick up the pieces. He hasn't been around much the last six months."

Grace nodded and took another very casual sip of her cocktail. "Good riddance to the harpy." She grimaced at whatever memory was replaying in her mind before visibly shaking it off. She looked back at

Lucy and me with a smile stretching back over her deep blue lips. "Enough about that mess. What is Douglas ordering us for dessert since he's stealing our appetizers?"

Douglas had a half-second hesitation like he saw her diversion tactic for what it was, but covered it with an answering smirk. "Now ladies, I will of course get you whatever it is that you desire, but please. I'm helping you finish these appetizers out of the good-ness of my heart."

We all laughed, but I couldn't help but gulp at the reminder that dating within this close-knit group was likely a mistake. They supported their friend and pushed out the interloper, and even if she deserved it, I didn't want to be the next harpy. I would keep my wandering eyes to myself going forward.

The rotating games of one-on-one pool started up. Joel convinced me to go up first while we waited for dessert and guided me through some shot place-ment. I got him to break, of course.

The running order had been decided while I was playing, and they were making me go twice because Grace wanted a chance to play Joel too. I was slated to play against Aaron. When I protested, I got shouted down. Apparently, I desperately needed the practice.

I picked a bite off the portion of bread pudding

LYNN CAMDEN

Douglas had ordered for me, swirled it in the accompanying crème anglaise, and took another fortifying sip of wine, delaying the inevitable humiliation at the pool table. My pulse started to kick up at the thought of facing Aaron across the table, which was ridiculous because I'd already decided not to flirt. We were going to have a perfectly neutral game of pool.

His texts in the group chat over the last week were easily identifiable. Always the most to-the-point, no emojis. Did I want to ogle someone who used full punctuation in his text? Surely not. It was for the best that I wasn't going to eye him anymore.

Joel smiled wickedly as he walked by me. "You're up, Evie."

58

Chapter Five

Aaron was already at the cues. He looked over at me with one brow raised, the quirk back at the corner of his mouth. I finished my bite and stood up, unsteady even though my heeled boots were chunky and stable. Maybe the glass of wine had gone to my head more than I'd thought.

Aaron was waiting for me as though he was content to stand there all day, but I hurried up and hustled over, smoothing my shirt over my hips. I thought I saw him follow my hands down over the bottom of my corset top, but I must have imagined it because when I looked at him, his eyes were focused somewhere around my hairline. He handed me a cue as I got to him.

"Here," he said abruptly. "This one's straighter and better for your height than what you had earlier."

"Oh?" I was surprised that he'd noticed. "And how can you tell?" He showed me the approximate height to look for, demonstrating with his where it should hit. I tried with mine. It was perfect. He'd measured me down to my heeled boots. I realized that we were close enough in height that my low heels brought my eyes level with his. He was so broad across that he'd seemed taller to me than he was.

"Thanks." I smiled at him. He was back to answering with nods, but he seemed pleased, a hint of a smile around his mouth. That lightning flash grin was hiding from me.

He gestured me to the table, and I walked ahead of him. When I got there, I turned to find him closer than I'd expected, throwing me off for the second time that night.

I shook it off and stared him directly in the eye, so close and level with mine. "I don't want to break. I will get stress hives if I have to do it again."

Under the brighter lights that spotlighted the pool table, his eyes looked brown, but I could see flecks and variations in them that the light wasn't bright enough to highlight. They looked at me with open amusement now, and that one dimple popped out. Even that much was enough to catch my breath.

"Evelyn," he said my name in a quick rush. "You'll never get more comfortable if you don't practice."

Was it my imagination, or was he getting looser and I getting jumpier as the evening wound on? He brushed past me, and the warmth of him imprinted briefly on my arm. He was a mini furnace, and I wanted to warm myself by my own personal bonfire.

He broke, thankfully, without pushing me further. I was so flustered I definitely would have flubbed it. He got stripes off the break, and soon it was my turn to start aiming for solids. The red ball seemed like a likely candidate, without much in the way, a straight line to the corner pocket.

The problem was it was an awkward placement and I had to lean way over the table, keeping one foot on the ground. I kept my chest out of the way with some contortionist moves, the flexible corset pushing my cleavage even higher as it rode up my waist. Aaron, to his credit, didn't stand around at the other end, where he would have had a clear view of my breast straining against my shirt, but instead stood nearby, helping me line up the shot with a quiet series of reminders and instruction.

His voice was low and calm in my ear as I got set up. "This is a tricky one. The angle is good, but your position on the table makes it harder. Remember to figure out your angle and follow through in a straight line even though your arm is out to the side."

With his coaching and some wild beginner's luck,

I managed it. It was the hardest shot I'd attempted yet. I eased off the table and grinned at him. He beamed back, twisting my stomach into knots, and I turned back to the game to escape it.

"What do you think I should go for next? Do I have a chance of getting the green? Your yellow looks like it might be in my way." That was probably not the right way to talk about pool balls, but he knew what I meant.

I pretended to study the table while sneaking sidelong looks at Aaron again. This solid tree of a man, rooted where I still felt adrift. He was intently focused on the table, considering my shots so carefully. He murmured options to me that I didn't even hear.

I refocused on the table and moved around it to set up the shot I'd picked at random just to put space between us. Aaron stayed where he was. If he looked down my shirt this time, I wouldn't blame him. Feeling dazed and wine-fuzzed, I bent over and got set up. My shoulders were back around my ears, my hand cramping tight around the cue. I thought I sensed the weight of his eyes, of everyone's eyes, on me, the bright lights of the table turning into a spotlight once again. My shot went wide, hitting his stripes instead of my solid. His murmur of encouragement or commiseration came from across the table, but I was just glad of the opportunity to draw back out from under the lights and lean against a nearby post under the guise of giving him space to play.

The intensity was back in his face, brows drawn and lips pursed as he studied the table and thought through his shot placement. His face looked more open every time I studied it, despite the focus in his deep-set eyes. I wasn't sure if he seemed more open because he was warming up to me, or because I was to him. Watching him line up his first shot had me stepping away from the post and hovering close to the table to see him sink his first easily.

He came around to get set up for his second and moved past me. I stepped out of his path too slowly, letting his broad arm brush against my chest. He might have flinched, but I jumped back like I'd held on to a live wire. Hoping that I hadn't been too much of a spectacle for our curious friends watching, I kept stepping backward until I hit the post again. From my safe place, I watched him sink his second shot but overshoot the placement for his third. He went back around the table and set up again. I realized he was purposefully making the hardest shots possible. He was perfectly lined up to take out his yellow stripe, but he was going for an awkward bank for the twelve.

I laughed out loud as I figured it out, stepping forward again to see the table more clearly. He paused, still stretched out over the table, thick arm in a perfect seven shape, swinging lightly from the hinge of his elbow.

My laugh caught in my throat as he looked up at me through his brows, the picture of him crouched and ready making the knot inside me twist tighter. I trailed off in a splutter, coughing. Now his brows quirked at me in concern.

I cleared my throat, remembered how to breathe, and answered those still raised, dark brown eyebrows directly. They seemed most in need of an answer.

"I'm fine. Sorry. I just realized you're soft-balling me."

The eyebrows rose higher. I addressed them again. "The balls remain hard." I paused to clear my throat once more, heat crawling over my neck. "The balls on the table, that is. But you. You are..." I searched for the word and finally found it. "Patronizing. You're deliberately picking tricky shots for yourself."

The eyebrows dismissed me and returned to their concentrating furrow. The cue resumed rubbing on his bearded chin while he started his precise swing. I was fascinated by his big hand in a bridge on the table, carefully arched to avoid interfering with other balls, thumb high to provide the perfect groove for the cue. He took that bank shot, balls clacking, and barely missed the corner pocket, making it my turn again. I groaned. I was hoping he'd clear the table and get it over with.

He unfolded and said, "It's less about patronizing, more like a handicap. It's not soft-balling either."

Had he emphasized "ball" ever so slightly? If so, maybe the ground would open up and disappear me?

He continued matter-of-factly, "It's about fairness."

He said it so simply, I was ready to accept it as truth. I didn't like being too agreeable with men on principle, but he moved on quickly, gesturing back to the table.

"What do you want to go for next? I think you've got a good chance at four or two."

I swallowed any further protest, and with his coaching, I picked my shot. When I leaned over, he made suggestions for my form and reminders of what to look for. I appreciated how he did it. He didn't crowd me or try to come up behind me and adjust my position. He talked me through it calmly, his voice an anchor under those hot lights, and I made the small adjustments that helped me line up my shot. I sunk it. And the next, with growing satisfaction. His quiet "Nice one" both times gave me a little extra glow.

In the end, he edged me out even while making his shots as tricky as he could. I appreciated that even with his self-imposed handicap, he was giving it his best effort. Not patronizing after all.

I clapped as he sunk the eight-ball, and he saluted me, tipping his cue in my direction. As we walked back to the table out of our cocooned glow, I could see my friends again—some deep in conversation, some watching us and cheering. Joel nudged Grace as he eyed me, but I refused to acknowledge whatever was happening there. At my seat, Aaron turned toward me. I hadn't noticed until then how he had walked me all the way back to my spot.

He gave me an open, happy smile, the biggest I'd seen on that surprisingly full mouth. I returned it automatically, stuck in a moment of mirroring him, caught up in looking him fully in the face, waiting for whatever he had to say.

"Thanks for the game," he said simply, and walked over to the bar to settle his bill.

I deflated from whatever it was I had been anticipating from him and joined in Lucy and Grace's conversation. Joel stood beside Grace's chair with his arm around her waist, leaning an elbow on the table, expression like a Cheshire cat. At second glance, all three were wearing almost identical grins. It was freaky, and I told them to stop immediately. Grace tucked her smile away and Lucy ducked her head to hide hers, but Joel kept on grinning, eyes twinkling at me, practically daring me to ask him what he was smiling about.

The best course was to pretend that he had never been born, but my cool look didn't impress him much, and Grace raised an eyebrow in response.

"Soooo..." Grace drew out that two-letter word for at least five syllables. "Great *game* you had." Her emphasis was an attack, as evidenced by Joel's snort and Lucy's quiet cackle. Lucy's eyes remained down, and Joel still had that shit-eating grin plastered on his face. I wondered where Douglas had gone and whether he could come save me from his boyfriend.

Grace continued. "Such *improvement* you showed. Aaron must be a great...*coach*." The other two were silently shaking with laughter beside her.

Joel wiped his eyes. "Evie, I do believe we'll make a pool player out of you yet."

I had no comeback, so I rolled my eyes and drained my lukewarm water glass, still at my spot on the table. That was the last time I'd play a game with Aaron, no matter how fun it had been. It wasn't worth getting flustered and teased, no matter how well-meaning the teasing.

Soon after, I was again bundled into Douglas's car, behind Joel in the passenger seat. He and Douglas were chatting about an old friend they had bumped into earlier in the day. It was comforting listening to them checking in, running down the day, and I could tell this was their regular routine.

I was glad for Aunt Bea, who always checked in with me. Otherwise, I might have felt lonely, listening at the keyhole of their relationship.

When we got to my place, they stayed parked out front to make sure I got in, and I waved as I unlocked my door. The kitchen lights were on to welcome me home. I didn't mind paying a little extra on my electricity bill if it meant not coming home to complete darkness.

My little upstairs apartment was cozy. The kitchen cabinets had been painted a pale yellow, setting off the white countertops and backsplash. The kitchen connected to the living/dining area, which was all one room. I'd set up a small, bright blue vintage table in the dining space, and my squashy couch in the living area. The couch was the only new purchase I'd made in my place other than my mattress. My bedroom and the bathroom were just down a short hall, and that was the whole place.

My landlady had let me know I could put some potted plants out in the shared patio outside, and I was looking forward to trying to grow a tomato plant in the spring. The tomatoes in the grocery store right now were hardly worth the name.

I went straight to my bedroom to change into my

sleep shirt and my fuzzy slippers. Even on chilly nights, I was a warm sleeper, so I couldn't wear too much to bed or I'd end up stripping out of it in the middle of the night. I had dishes in the sink, but my bed was practically begging me to fall into it, so I trekked back to the kitchen to turn off the light and check the locks on all the windows and doors before brushing my teeth and doing my evening skincare.

I was snuggled under the covers within fifteen minutes of getting home, a fall spice candle lit and my bedside lamp throwing a small circle of yellow light.

I considered picking up my e-reader. Sarah MacLean had a new book out, and I'd been waffling between buying it or waiting for a sale. The hold on it at the library was long. But it was getting too late to start something new, even for a weekend.

I lay back and started to do the body scan meditation I did most nights, relaxing each part of me in succession while slowing my exhales and softening my breath. I started at my toes and worked my way up, releasing stress gradually as I went.

I was starting to go fuzzy with sleep and considering turning off my lights when a pair of big, rough hands popped into my mind. I opened my eyes, completely alert again, and shook my head. I banished the hands from my mind, and I returned to my meditation. I was scanning my arms when the hands came back and took away all my focus.

Strong hands, grabbing my elbow to steady me; thick eyebrows, demanding a response; broad shoulders, brushing past me and sending heat into my body. I was tense, undoing all my careful breathwork, practically panting.

The heat of him was a bonfire in my memory. The hands were roving now, the grip firmer and more possessive, curling around my inner thigh and making me sweat. The brows were lowered, glaring at me with fierce concentration.

My imagination had gone rogue and was making me ache. I scrambled for the vibes in my bedside table drawer, needing to release the tension. I needed penetration, needed to feel full and taken over. I set my dildo on low vibration, and it slid inside easily, I was so slick. The smaller vibe's suction cup went right above my clit. I was starting to sweat, a drip running between my breasts. I couldn't remember the last time I'd been so turned on, and was torn between making it last or coming at once.

But I was keyed up and ready, and started upping the vibration without conscious thought. I pictured rough hands playing gently with my clit, contrasting with thick fingers thrusting in with absolute authority, broad shoulders spreading my thighs wide, and eyebrows raised and commanding me to come. Those fingers curled inside me. I whimpered, and my body twisted into a tight C as I came, bucking when the vibration got too intense for my now-sensitive clit. I turned it off quickly.

The orgasm had wrung out all my muscle tension better than any meditation had ever tried. As long as I didn't think about who I had masturbated to. I wouldn't think about it. My brain was officially offline. I barely had the presence of mind to put away my vibrators and blow out my candle before I was asleep.

Chapter Six

The gray of early October resolved into weather that was crisp, clear-skied, and getting colder by the day. The threat of snow hung in the air. I had abandoned my wool coat in favor of a puffy jacket I bought at the mall while I waited for my heavy-duty winter coat. Most people I saw on the street were still wearing light jackets, but I had not yet developed my winter tolerance for the prairies. I hadn't seen my new friends, or Aaron, since that night weeks ago that I definitely never thought about.

I had woken up the next day and stuffed all thoughts about hands and brows into a large black box in my mind and then sat on it to close it, locked it with a padlock, and shoved it into a cellar in the recess of my brain. I was determined it would stay there. I was too busy for anything else.

My major events projects were all focused on the holidays. There were exactly fourteen different banquets, luncheons, and concerts we were involved in planning. All of it would be done by the middle of December. Marketing was underway for some, invites sent for others, and sign-up sheets posted for a few that were smaller on-campus affairs.

I was already run ragged, and it was only mid-October. I knew had to treat it as a marathon, but I'd been going at a sprint pace. Checking for new emails at four a.m. when I couldn't sleep wasn't helping anyone, I knew. But I couldn't stop. Joel had practically begged me the last time I sent him an email in the middle of the night to turn off my email, unkindly pointing out that the bags under my eyes were starting growing bags.

The mirror agreed with Joel, unfortunately. My dark circles were a permanent bruise, and I could see my skin getting grayer and saggier by the day, despite any number of potions and lotions I tried. I needed sleep. My mind whirled at all times, lists dancing in my head, to-dos popping up like ground squirrels just as I was about to drift off.

Grace had practically bullied me into coming for a midweek dinner at the pub. I hadn't been able to make any weekend pub dates, with working late and sheer exhaustion winning every time I thought of going out. But, as Grace said, I had to eat. I could go, laugh with friends, release some stress, keep away from my phone, and hopefully fall into a deep, peaceful sleep later. Hopefully.

The moon was already out when I hopped up the three steps that took me into the pub and breathed in deep, the warm, moist air heating me from the inside out. The lights were low as usual, and our usual server, Julia, waved at me and pointed in the direction of the table around the corner of the bar. I took the time to hang my coat, thankful for some time to catch my breath. I didn't mind walking in the chill—it helped keep my stress at bay—but walking in the dark always made me jumpy and increased my pace, until my breath couldn't keep up with my legs.

The greetings of my friends warmed me as I slid into the booth. A hot toddy was waiting at my spot, steam curling decadently above it. I smiled gratefully at Grace after I gave her a hug and waved around the table.

"Thanks so much. I definitely need the warm-up tonight."

She smiled back, but her eyes held a mischievous light. She looked like she could barely contain herself. I raised my brow in question at her.

"Don't thank me, Evie. Aaron ordered it for you tonight. He said with the wind you would need it right when you got in." There was mischief dancing in her eyes.

"Oh!" I was already flustered, and the night had just begun.

I looked over at Aaron, who appeared to be examining his menu carefully. The menu that he had to have completely memorized by now after coming here for years. What did he have to look over? He ordered shepherd's pie almost every time. Looking closer, his head was cocked like he was listening.

I glanced around the table. Lucy was examining her nail polish, and Joel was checking a text. Douglas was MIA tonight, and I remembered Joel mentioning he had a work event this evening. Everyone looked very casual and deeply absorbed in anything except the conversation at hand.

I was determined to be poised.

"Thanks so much, Aaron!" Too chipper, perhaps. I scaled it back. "You were right. The wind today is killer, and this is the perfect drink to sit down to." I ended with a smile that was hopefully not as unhinged as I felt inside.

He set down his menu and looked back at me. "You're welcome," he said simply. He continued in a rush. "Now that it's colder and darker, you should let

75

one of us pick you up from work. The temperature always drops in the evening, and in the dark, it's harder to see ice on the sidewalk."

He saw me gaping at him, and his brows furrowed. "You're on my way to the pub. I can easily come by and get you."

I was not going to look around the table again. I was not even going to try to catch Joel's eye. "Well, I like the walk, but maybe you're right. I'm always a little jumpier at night."

Concern took over Aaron's whole face, and his stare got so intense I didn't know where to look. I hated prolonged eye contact.

"Do you not feel safe on your walk? Has anyone ever bothered you? Is it well lit? Do you carry a whistle?" His questions were rapid-fire. He was still looking directly into my eyes.

I would not be intimidated by his deep-set stare. "I'm fine. It's well lit, and no one bothers me. I have a whistle." I sat back, proud of myself for not crumbling under the pressure. This was another difference since I'd moved to a smaller city. The streets were more deserted at night, and all my friends drove. They couldn't fathom why someone would walk home in the dark. I picked up my delicious warm drink and lifted it in his direction in a silent "Cheers." With a small smile, I took my first sip and reveled in the warmth sliding down my throat and radiating out from my center.

His eyes were still on me, with the remnants of worry still visible on his face, but now his dark brows had a different slant to their usual furrow, and something new I couldn't name sparked in his eyes. I turned away, breaking our too-intimate stare, and looked around the table again.

Joel, Grace, and Lucy had all dropped any pretense of not paying attention and were watching our exchange like they had popcorn in one hand and candy in the other. The spotlight was back, and it was not imagined either.

"So," I said, putting extra fake sweetness in my voice and glaring around at my friends, "what's everyone ordering tonight?"

Joel jumped his eyes back to his menu at once. Grace smirked at me before saying, "I think I'll have the vindaloo today. Extra spicy."

Julia came over right on cue and took everyone's order. I decided on butter chicken, medium spice. They had great naan, and I ordered extra on the side so I'd have enough for tomorrow's lunch. Aaron of course got the shepherd's pie, unwittingly proving me right.

Aaron ordered an appetizer of scotch eggs for the table after he heard me and Grace discussing them.

I'd seen them before, but they looked and sounded so odd, I'd never tried them. They came with chutney for dipping. "You have to just try them," he explained after he put in the order. "They're weird as a concept, but they're better than they sound."

They were so hot when they came to the table that we all had to wait before we could dig in, and we each grabbed a half egg with our fingers. Once I took my first bite, I understood what Aaron meant. They had a crispy crumb exterior and a juicy, savory meat layer, deeply spiced, and then an egg at the center. What wasn't to like? It was like eating a whole breakfast in one bite—eggs, sausages, and toast. The chutney was sweet and spicy and delicious, pairing well with the egg.

Grace and I danced in our seats, and Aaron watched us with a smile. His was gone while we were still on our first bites.

"I take it you like it?" Aaron was addressing me, but Lucy jumped in with a cheeky "Delicious!" She gave me a wink across the table that Aaron couldn't see from his seat beside her.

I gave her a tiny shake of my head. She'd been texting me more outside of the group chat in the last few weeks and dropping not-so-subtle hints about me and Aaron getting together. She was probably texting him the same kinds of things. I was only surprised that she hadn't said anything outright in the group chat. On that day I would sink into the ground and then block her number from my earthly grave.

"Yes, they're very good." I took another bite to keep from saying anything more.

While we waited for our main courses to arrive, the conversation turned to work, with Aaron and Lucy asking questions, and Joel, Grace, and me venting about how busy it had been.

"It's a nice campus, though. Sometimes I miss it. It's pretty in the fall too." Aaron had a faraway look before focusing on me again. "What do you think of it?"

"It's been good. People are nice, the cafeterias and cafes are great, and I'm only lost every other week now." I smiled, and his tiny grin quirked the corner of his mouth in response. "I'm not used to the academic world, though. That's been an adjustment. A couple of college night classes aren't the same."

I flashed back to those dingy gray walls and flickering florescent lights, and the awkwardness of new classmates and icebreaker questions. I'd only made it through three classes before giving it up. I'd been slowly shaking off my inferiority complex the more time I spent on campus.

Aaron said, "Academia isn't all it's cracked up to

be. If you have good employment and job satisfaction, that's all you really need."

I nodded, appreciating Aaron making the effort to validate me when I was the only person there without a degree. "Well, I can now say I've met PhDs that can't problem-solve their way out of a paper bag, so I guess it's not everything. You should have heard me walking Dr. Schultz through filling out an online form and clicking 'Submit.'" Aaron chuckled, and I continued. "All of the steps were laid out in my initial email! I don't think he even read it."

"I wonder when you're going to give up on that procedure," Joel interjected. "You would save time by taking down their information yourself and filling in the forms for them."

"Right, but you have to train people how to follow the procedure, or you get nowhere. If I put the work in this year, maybe next year they'll send in their event forms automatically." I was building a system for future events teams that I didn't even know if I'd be a part of. I would likely have moved on to something new by then. Suddenly I was exhausted. "Plus, there are younger and younger department heads coming up through the ranks all the time, and even older people can learn new tech if they want to. I just taught my Aunt Bea hashtagging last week."

I smiled to myself at the memory. She was relentlessly hashtagging every text she sent me now, to my endless amusement. Her hashtags were always full sentences. The most recent one was:

Have a good day! 😈 *#itscoldbutatleastthesunisoutandthesidewalksaredry* 🖤 💀

She killed me every time. I knew she actually understood the concept, but she liked messing with me.

Our food came, and the conversation lulled. My butter chicken was too hot to eat, but I nibbled the naan and thought again about work. My weekly battles with Dr. Gossman and her dogged assistant in Social Work continued, as I tried to keep them from shooting for the moon on a Ryanair budget.

Joel surprised me by turning to Aaron and saying, "Aaron, talk some sense into Evie. She can't keep running herself ragged at work, or she won't last through the month!"

Joel and Grace had been chastising me for not sleeping yet again. I could only listen to their scolding so many times. There was absolutely nothing I could do about my schedule, my workload, or my sleep. I'd been trying to wind down every night. I was starting to get resentful about their constant badgering.

There was nothing Aaron could say or do to make me magically sleep—don't think about that one night, Evie, don't go there—but he squared his shoulders across from me, ready to give it his best shot.

"Evelyn. I run my own business," he began. I was still vague on the details, but I knew it was some sort of construction company. I ignored the shiver from hearing my full name in his deep voice and nodded back at him.

"Sustainability is important in business. I can't run my business if it's running me. At the end of every day, before I clock out for the day, I look at my task list. I write down everything and anything that's on my mind. Then I prioritize." He started ticking off points on his big fingers, not aware of their effect on me, or where I had been imagining using them. I blinked back into focus.

"I ask myself: does this need to be done at all, and when do I need to do it? Once I decide, I look at my time blocks for the week and schedule it on my calendar." His fingers picked up his fork again, and he waved it at me to emphasize his next point. "Once all my tasks are scheduled, I pack it away and don't look at it again until the next morning. I don't check email, I don't answer my work line unless I'm on call for a crew, I decompress." His fork stabbed toward me at every word now. "You need to set boundaries. No one else can do that for you."

Apparently done his speech, he scooped another chunk of mashed potato and kept eating like the issue had been completely solved. Grace, Joel, and even Lucy were nodding along like the church choir at a sermon. He had them convinced at least.

As I mulled it over, I could see the sense in what he said, but instead of focusing on his advice, I was focusing on his overconfidence. Had he really just made a pronouncement based on what he did and expected it would fix everything for me? I thought as I ate, checking out of the conversation completely. Grace gave up trying to draw me back into it, and when Aaron caught my eye later, I looked back to my plate. He wasn't wrong, necessarily, but I could not get over how certain he was that he had all the answers. I would have liked to be that certain about anything in my life. I was just trying to decide if it was hot or irritating. Maybe both.

After the bills were settled and leftovers packed, and everyone had said at least three rounds of good-byes, we all got up from the table. Aaron stopped me on the way to the coatroom with that big hand on my arm again. Even though he didn't tower over me, his presence always made it feel like he did, shoulders blocking out the rest of the room, drawing me to look at him and forget the rest of the world. He waited until my eyes had made the short trip up to his, catching on his neat beard and full mouth.

Bad Evie. We do not stare at our friends' or acquaintances' mouths. We probably also do not picture them while masturbating. Oops.

"I'm taking you home," he said, once our eyes had connected at last. When he saw me open my mouth, he shook his head firmly, a swift cut to the left nipping my protests in the bud. "You're on my way, and my truck is already heating. It'll be toasty for you." Again, the utter certainty with this one. Maybe one day I would see him uncertain, desperate, and fumbling.

A preheated vehicle was too much to pass up, and his hand on my arm was very convincing, the gentle touch lighting up my nerve endings, reminding me how touch-deprived I was. I pictured him sliding down my arm to intertwine our fingers and blushed. My previously unknown hand fetish was getting out of control. I nodded at him, not trusting myself to speak.

We said our final round of goodbyes with hugs to our friends, zipped into our jackets, tucked scarves around our faces, and headed out into the cold. Grace sang with Lucy as they walked to Grace's car. I was the only one in the group without a car, and I was starting to feel pathetic about all the rides people felt they had to give me.

We stopped where Aaron's truck sat on the street. Huge and black, it blended into the night except where the streetlights gleamed on its polished surface. He walked with me to the passenger side and stopped with his hand on the handle, our breath mingling in a fog in front of us.

"Hang on a sec, I need to move my drop sheet." He lightly leaped up, folded up a cloth that was spread over the whole passenger side, and tossed it in the back. He stepped down and motioned me past him. His hand under my elbow steadied as I got in. Such a polite boy. The truck didn't have that lower step that made it easier to climb in.

Settling in with my boxed leftovers tucked in beside me, I realized the seat was warmer than the truck temperature. The leather radiated its heat up my lower back, and I relaxed into its welcoming cocoon. In the short time it took him to walk around the truck, I had already started to drift. I was so tired. I started when his door slammed, and quickly put my seatbelt on. He buckled in and turned to me.

"Joel said you live on Elm. What's your address?" His voice was soft, and I was tempted to sink into its quiet rumble the way my ass was currently sinking into the heated seats.

I pulled myself together enough to give him directions, and he began the short trip toward my place. The silence was something I wasn't used to when being dropped off, and he didn't seem inclined to fill it. Getting a ride with Douglas and Joel meant I always had conversation in the front to listen to, with the option of participating if I wanted. Now I had to come up with something to say.

"Why did you have a sheet in the front seat?" I blurted out the first inane thing that came to mind.

"I put a drop sheet over my seats during the day while I'm in work clothes. I move it over once I've changed. I get very dirty, and I don't want to grind stone dust into the truck seats."

I made a noise that must have sounded very interested because he continued.

"I don't even go into the house in my work clothes," he said, "I put them straight into the washer in the garage when I get home. I even have a utility sink in the garage to get the worst of the dust off my hair and face so I don't track too much through the house on my way to the shower."

I couldn't think of anything that would get someone that filthy. "What do you do to get so dusty?"

He looked at me, surprised, and gave a wry half chuckle. "I'm a stonemason. I rebuild old limestone foundations and do other stonework like retaining walls and decorative stone structures. I did that limestone and concrete marker for the boulevard on Main Street." He gave me another sidelong glance at the next stop sign. "You didn't ask Joel or Grace about me?"

Did he sound hurt that I hadn't been researching his entire history? "Sorry, I'm not a private eye." I said it lightly and watched the side of his face quirk up in a grin. "I just thought from what Grace said that you worked in construction. I was picturing you building houses."

"You'd look pretty cute in a Sherlock Holmes hat." He tossed it off casually, unaware of the bombs it set off in my psyche. He frowned, thinking, as he made another turn. "What are those hats called, anyway?"

I was still paused on "cute" and couldn't form rational thought. "I don't know. Something with deer in the name. Deerhunter? You'll have to look it up." My flirting ability was on the fritz if that was the best I could do.

We were already at my place, and I couldn't think of a single excuse to invite him in or somehow prolong our time together. He pulled up to the curb with his hazards flashing, taking up most of the lane.

Aaron turned his whole upper body toward me,

the truck idling. One arm draped over the wheel, the other braced on the seat back next to me. His shoulders filled the cab. His stare was intense again in the dim light from the streetlamps. Was he going to put some moves on me? Did I want him to?

"Listen," he said seriously, "I hope I didn't upset you with my speech earlier. You don't have to do anything I do. I went through a stage when I was starting my business where I was killing myself with stress and never took any breaks from work. I just... don't want to see any of my friends make the same mistakes I did." He blew out a breath. "Well. Anyway. I'm sorry if it was too much. You'll figure out what works best for you."

Oh, so no moves. That was fine. I didn't need moves. I mustered up a reassuring smile and my lightest tone. Maybe he was less sure of himself than what he projected. Call him out on being overbearing, or let it go? I thought he could take it well, like Joel had, but suddenly I wasn't sure.

"Don't worry about it. I'm thinking about what you said." I stopped talking before I could get too honest with him. I didn't want to examine getting too hung up on being called a "friend." Perhaps he always texted his buddies about women he just wanted to be friends with. Maybe he had an extensive vetting process for friendship. I reminded myself firmly that

I didn't want anything else from him, despite what my fantasizing indicated.

"Oh, one more thing. I know you're busy, but Joel said you'd be the perfect person to brainstorm with about what I should do for my crew for the holidays. Every year I've thought about throwing a party, but I never get around to it. Can I text you some time for some advice?" He sounded tentative, as he might well, after lecturing me on how busy I was. "You don't have to do anything, I just need a few ideas. I promise it'll only take a few minutes."

"No problem. You have my number. Thanks for the ride, I appreciate it." I unbuckled myself and opened the door as I spoke. "See you next week maybe?"

As I walked off I saw him still waiting at the curb, not concerned about the car coming up behind him, watching to make sure I got in okay. When my door opened and I waved at him, he waved back and drove away.

Chapter Seven

I toed off my boots and hung my jacket in the tiny mudroom off the kitchen, picked up my backpack where I'd dumped it earlier, put my lunch containers in the kitchen, and did a quick five-minute cleanup. Then I headed straight to my room for my comfiest high-waisted leggings and a bralette. I added a zip-up sweater overtop to stay warm and rooted around in the bottom of my sock drawer and found my fuzziest socks. I was nearly ready to watch some mindless TV before bed.

I had just finished my evening skincare and was all shiny and fresh when I heard a soft knock at my door.

It had to be Aaron. Or a murderer. No one else would be in my area at this hour. I walked over and saw Aaron through the glass panes, lit up by my exterior light fixture.

When I unlocked the door and opened it, the cold swept in in a big gust over the threshold. I stood back so he could come in without letting all of the outdoors in with him. He stepped in and shut the door quickly.

"Sorry," he said, addressing my shoulder. I looked down to the left. My sweater was zipped up most of the way but had slipped off one shoulder. The pinky-red lace of my bralette was on display. I twitched the sweater back since he was obviously distracted. His eyes jumped to my dewy face.

"Sorry," he said again. We seemed doomed to repeat this moment, trapped in a mini Groundhog Day.

"What's up, Aaron?" I asked as gently as possible, hoping to break him out of this cycle.

"Oh!" He held up the box with my leftovers. "You left these in the truck. I didn't see them till I hit the end of the street. Then I had to turn around and find parking, but this area is crammed full, so I went five blocks over to find a spot big enough for the truck and then walked over and..." He petered off, probably realizing that he was rambling.

I nearly laughed. It was the most flustered I'd ever

seen him. He was cute this way and would be easy to tease. But I didn't want to embarrass him, and I was thankful he'd gone to so much trouble to bring my leftovers.

"Sorry about that. It's my fault for forgetting them again." I motioned to the coat hook. "Do you want to come in for a bit and warm up before you walk back? I have tea, hot chocolate, or wine. I think I even have some spiced rum."

He started taking off his jacket as I spoke, without hesitation. I liked that we didn't have to go back and forth with any "Oh, I wouldn't want to bother you," "Oh, it's no trouble at all," or "Well, if you're sure..." nonsense. He just jumped on the invitation eagerly. His boots joined mine on the rack, hanging over the edge. He followed me into the kitchen on socked feet and stood there, taking in my place.

I hadn't had many people over. Grace had hung out here a few times, and Joel and Douglas had helped with the couch and stayed long enough for a coffee. Usually, I found it cozy, but Aaron's broad shoulders made my kitchen feel cramped.

"What do you want to drink?" I asked, waving toward the options lined up on the counter. He chose a lemony tea, and I shooed him into the living room to get comfortable while I made it. I made the same for myself and put away my leftovers while it steeped.

When I brought the tea in, he was fully sprawled on my couch, one leg up on the chaise, arms spread along the back, the picture of relaxation. I lifted an eyebrow to see him so at ease and set his tea within reach, retreating to the armchair across from him. He leaned further back, obviously comfortable in my space. Having him here, by himself, made that feeling of being under the microscope dissipate so thoroughly, I couldn't marshal any reason not to openly lust after him. There was no friend group here to watch or judge.

Warmth spread through me, and an itchy feeling pricked alongside it. He looked too relaxed. I wanted him as on edge as I felt. I wanted to see the Aaron who'd lost his mind and train of thought at the door earlier. The glimpse of that Aaron had both intrigued me and put me on solid ground. Lust and uncomplicated need, that was something I understood.

While his eyes were on my bookshelf, I eased my sweater zipper down, and when his gaze wandered back to me, I took the opportunity to reach for my teacup, giving him a generous flash of my cleavage and the lacy bralette he'd been admiring earlier. I heard what might have been a grunt and hid my satisfied smirk with my teacup. I blew on the surface of my tea and let my sweater slouch down one shoulder again, the raspberry lace visible right down to the top of my breast.

"How's your tea?" I asked sweetly, still staring into my cup.

His voice was gruff. "It's too hot to try, Ev."

That nickname in that voice brought color to my cheeks. I lifted my eyes to his, needing to see his face. It was pained, his eyes tracing the line of lace down to where it disappeared under my sweater. I could almost feel his gaze on my bare shoulder and along my collarbone and down to the generous swell of my breast. His slouch was not at all relaxed now. One hand gripped the couch, and the other was curled into a fist on his knee.

I took a painful sip of my tea. It hadn't cooled enough to drink, but I needed something to do so I didn't jump over the coffee table, straddle his big thighs, and see for myself what those hands could do.

"If you blow on it, it should be cool enough," I said, my voice throaty and my words more suggestive than I'd intended.

He smirked at my word choice and seemed to shake off his tension with a shrug of his shoulders. He leaned forward to pick up his tea. He took a small sip and cast his eyes around my room again, obviously looking for a distraction.

"Who's in the picture on your bookshelf?" He nodded at the picture of the three generations of Stone women on the shelf across the room.

"That's my mom, my Aunt Bea, and my granny." I smiled a little sadly at how happy we'd been that day, celebrating my tenth birthday, before the losses had piled up. He was still looking at the frame, making it easier to keep talking. "My granny died of breast cancer two years after that picture. The same cancer took my mom when I was nineteen. My Aunt Bea is on the far right. She's still around, lives on the East Coast. She keeps tabs on me, and I do the same for her." I shook away the lump of tears I felt creeping up my throat.

Aaron leaned forward, his eyes intense and so full of sympathy I had to look back down at my cup. "I'm sorry," he said simply.

I nodded and didn't trust myself to elaborate any further. I took another sip of tea, swallowing down my tears and my sadness. I'd shed enough tears for a lifetime in my teens. On my twentieth birthday, I'd said I was done crying. Aunt Bea had insisted neither life nor tears worked like that, but I'd been adamant. And so far, I'd been steadfast. I'd managed another ten years without breaking down. If a movie got too sad, I left. If I got frustrated at work, I paced around until I got it out of my system. The only tears on my cheeks were the ones the icy wind coaxed out on my morning walks, and those didn't count.

Aaron leaned back again, his eyes still intent on my face. "What about your dad?"

"Oh, it's something of a family tradition not to bother with those." My smile felt lopsided. He had maneuvered us beyond the bounds of easy lust, and I couldn't see a clear path back. He raised an eyebrow for me to continue.

"I suspect my granny had a husband, but she never talked about him. She never talked about why she left England with two tiny children, and she never talked about her family there. I think she must have been running. It must have been something awful for her to leave with nothing and start over on the other side of the world."

I took another sip. "My mom was pretty independent too. All the Stone women are. She had a fling, got pregnant, and raised me on her own. I don't think she ever told the guy. I don't think she wanted him involved."

"Were you ever curious about him?"

"Sometimes, when I was little. But not often as I grew up. Some of the kids in high school were split between their divorced parents. That always seemed rough to me, like the kids were scraps for parents to fight over. I learned to appreciate what I had."

"So your aunt didn't marry either?"

"No." I paused. "I think she has a long-term lover, though. It's not a topic we go into."

Aaron seemed to sense I'd shared as much as I was willing. "My parents are outside the city. Farmers. They do grain and vegetable shares. My sister Alice lives near them. She's got farming in the blood too, and married a farmer. Their farm does mostly dairy, some grain. I'm the proud uncle to two holy terrors. I don't see them as much as I'd like, but at least they're only an hour away."

I smiled at the image of him growing up with hay in his hair. "Did you want to be a farmer when you were little? Was your family disappointed when you weren't?"

He grinned back at me. "My grandfather, my dad's dad, was a stonemason. He used to take me with him whenever I could get out of helping my parents with chores. I loved watching him rebuild a wall, how he had to figure out which stones to remove to keep the structural integrity while he rebuilt a section."

He petered off, but I wanted to hear more. "How did you learn to do it? Did he teach you?"

"I learned some from watching him and helping

him, but he was retiring when I was ready to apprentice. The apprenticeship takes time. The trade is old and not taught as thoroughly in North America, so I went to Europe to finish my training. I think my parents knew from early on that the stone was calling me."

"Wow, I can't imagine being called to a career from such a young age. How did the business school thing fit into that? That's where you met everyone, right?"

"Right. Well, my parents said regardless of what I wanted to do, I had to get an undergrad. They were hoping I'd take agriculture, but business seemed the most relevant." He laughed. "If I'd known how the faculty was, I might have done a philosophy major instead."

"Why, what's wrong with business?"

"It's image-focused, and you get points for how much schmoozing, wheeling, and dealing you're doing. Business smarts are associated with being charismatic and the loudest person in the room. I was never that guy. But I learned the tools I needed. Being pushed into socializing didn't kill me, even if it was draining."

I could picture him sitting in a corner, working up the energy to socialize and check off the boxes he thought he was missing. "Joel and Douglas aren't shallow and schmoozy. I can't imagine it at all."

"Well, university days aren't really a showcase for your best self. All of us were masking who we were. Douglas wasn't out, and Joel was only out to a few people. You haven't met Chris yet, but he was a huge player, always making moves and partying. It was encouraged, rewarded. And so I was way more out there too. It cost me, though. I almost didn't finish my degree, I was so burnt out."

I nodded, and he continued, "When I think about it, it's amazing that we managed to stay friends at all. But once we lived together, that's when we started to bond."

I'd never really had a group like that. My school years had been so caught up in Mum, in doctor's appointments, in getting food boxes from church basements, and applying for aid from different government programs. It was just me and Mum and Aunt Bea. I was an island. Aaron was something else. A peninsula maybe, still connected to the mainland.

I wanted him to keep talking. "And after university, you did your apprenticeship?"

"Yes. I went to Italy for part of it. My Italian still sucks, but I can order at a restaurant in Sicily and not embarrass myself. I worked with some relatives of my grandfather's. They taught me everything I know."

"Do you miss it? It must be beautiful there." I suddenly ached for all the lost moments of my teens and twenties. This was what my peers were doing as I scrounged and worked and got back on my feet after losing my whole world. They were traveling to places with olive trees and vineyards and fooling around and partying with housemates and getting through university courses together and complaining about tough profs.

I saw glimpses of that life every day on campus. Students gossiping arm in arm, crying in the bathroom, bleary-eyed, and frantically taking notes in the pods at the library. I envied them all, small as it made me.

"I loved it there," he said, drawing me back to the present. "But the most beautiful scenery in the world isn't everything. My home is here, with my friends and family, doing work I love, and braving the cold for seven months of the year." He raised his mug at me.

I was not looking forward to the deep freeze everyone teased me with. I had been so young when we lived here last, I couldn't remember what a prairie winter felt like.

"Speaking of which, I should get going. Early start tomorrow." He rose as he spoke, and I followed him up as though pulled on a string.

"What time do you get to work?" I was stalling.

"I get to work around six-thirty. I get up at five. My guys are at the jobsite by seven-thirty or eight depending on where we're working, and I like to get my paperwork done first thing."

My jaw dropped. "My work hours are eight-thirty to four-thirty, and usually I think that's too early." I was not a morning person.

He took his cup into the kitchen. "Just leave it in the sink. I'll run my dishwasher tomorrow," I called after him.

I yanked my sweater back into place irritably and followed him. After the satisfying initial reaction it got, it might as well have been his grandmother's shoulder for all he looked at it.

He'd already stamped on his boots and had his coat in hand. His rush made me worry that I'd interrogated him for too long.

"Thanks for warming me up, Evelyn," He zipped up his light jacket as he spoke. He didn't have a scarf, and his throat under his short, neat beard was exposed. I hoped he would be warm enough. "Oh, hey, I almost forgot. I'm going to be near campus next week Wednesday for an estimate. I was thinking of swinging by and seeing if you and Joel and Grace want to go for lunch. Are you free?"

I took my phone out of my sweater pocket and

pulled up my calendar. "Yes, I don't have any meet-ings. I can block off some time for a longer lunch."

"Great." He looked like I'd made his whole week. I smiled back, heart lifting at the thought. He stepped closer to me and reached out a hand as though to touch me, but stopped short. The moment stretched out, his hand still up, my face turned up to him, his face now hard to read, cast in shadow by the door light coming in through the window behind him.

"See you next week" was all he said. He dropped his hand and went out into the windy night, and I locked the door behind him on autopilot. The click of the lock brought me down to earth. I shook my head and finished getting ready for bed.

I lay awake for a while processing all of our inter-actions. I didn't understand my outsized reaction to Aaron. I'd never before experienced this kind of gut-clenching restlessness around a man. From him, all it took was a look or two to send me spiraling into lust and anticipation. Every time we interacted, a spring inside me wound tighter until I didn't know how it didn't snap. Where would all this tension lead? I could not let it spin me into something out of my control.

I sighed out loud, or maybe it was a groan. Did he

want me? Did it matter? There was at least one thing I knew for certain. He had stared at my bra. Twice. He had been checking me out.

Another thing I knew for certain? I wanted him to do it again.

Chapter Eight

Wednesday morning rolled around, and for some reason that I refused to examine, I'd chosen to wear an off-white cropped cowl neck sweater that set off my collarbones—a very good feature of mine, if I did say so myself—and a bra that gave me a lot of lift but was annoying to wear. The straps were barely on my shoulders, and when I moved, I had to subtly adjust them. I didn't have any particular reason for wearing such a finicky bra to work. I also had a high-waisted pencil skirt on, and my ass looked amazing. Also for no particular reason. It was not the most fun to do a lot of walking in, but I'd be mostly in my office all day. Except for lunch.

The bags under my eyes had been well wrangled with concealer, and I was hoping my pink lipstick struck a balance between day-appropriate and sexy. I'd gotten a wolf whistle from Grace when I walked in, so I wasn't sure where the balance scales tipped.

At eleven forty-five, I heard Aaron's deep voice and our admin's high laugh.

Grace poked her head into my office. "Are you coming out? Aaron is here."

"Yes, I'll be right there," I called, snatching up my bag.

When I got to the front desk, Aaron was standing in front of it, dressed as I'd never seen him before. His jeans were worn and had white and gray splotches on them. His thick, long-sleeved shirt had his company logo "DeLuca Stone Works" embroidered on the chest, and it too had splotches all over. His jacket was over one arm, and he was wearing a matching branded black toque and thick steel-toed boots. He looked like he could kick through walls. Hell, he probably did.

"Hey," he said as I walked up.

"Hey to you," I said, giving him a small wave. I realized that I'd never seen him in the bright light of day. His eyes were a flecked hazel brown with a ring of lighter color at the center. They looked like they would shift in every light, in every mood, with every color he wore. They intrigued me as much as the rest of him.

Those eyes were on me now, taking in my exposed collarbones, my cropped sweater, my calf-length tight skirt. My curves were on full display today, and from the looks of it, he liked what he saw.

Grace stood by the front desk, but she didn't have her coat. She looked at us both apologetically.

"I'm so sorry, you two," she said, "I'd love to join you for lunch today, but Melanie and I have a teleconference that we need to dial in to. We'll be eating our lunch in the boardroom today. And of course, Joel had that meeting with the English dean that he couldn't get out of."

That caught me off guard. "Really? Why didn't you tell me earlier? And Joel. He went for that meeting at ten, and I assumed he'd be back by now." I hoped that Aaron didn't think I'd orchestrated this. I was getting a weird vibe from Melanie's extremely blank expression, which made me think that Grace's meeting might not exist.

Aaron stepped in gracefully, maybe alarmed by Grace and me eyeing each other. I tried projecting my suspicions directly into her eyeballs, but she refused to cave under pressure.

"That's too bad, Grace. Can we bring you and Melanie anything from Cordera? Dessert? A reward for surviving your conference?" He sounded so genuinely disappointed that Grace couldn't come, I wasn't sure whether to be relieved or offended.

No, enough self-doubt. If he didn't want to see me, he wouldn't have come in the other night, and he wouldn't have initiated a lunch date.

I threw another suspicious glare at Grace as we headed out. We hadn't had our first snow yet, but we'd had an extremely hazardous bout of freezing rain that had turned all of the sidewalks into skating rinks. It was another reason I'd taken the bus to work. The university had salted the entrances, but treacherous patches of ice still held on stubbornly.

His giant gleaming truck had its hazards on in the loading zone in front of the admin building. As soon as I saw it, I felt ridiculous. This skirt was not going to make vaulting into his truck easy.

I turned to Aaron. "Do you mind lending me a hand again?"

His firm grip on my elbow was entirely necessary this time. I had to slide my skirt up past my knees, and barely made it in, even with his help. The tights I was wearing underneath were thick enough that I didn't worry about flashing him, but it was absolutely mortifying to struggle.

"Sorry about the truck," he said, sliding easily into his seat. "It's not very friendly for fancy office attire. I should add the running boards back on for you. I figured it would be better to take it than walk across campus and waste most of your lunch hour."

That he was thinking about both altering his truck for me and about how much time I had for lunch gave me pause. I noticed that he had the drop cloth over his side, but he'd already cleared my seat. The back was empty too. He must have been expecting us all to pile into the truck and had prepared ahead of time. He really was thoughtful.

"So, Cordera's? I haven't made it there yet, but I hear it's great." I buckled in, and he started up the truck and clicked on the seat warmer for me, even though the interior was still warm from his drive.

"Yeah, it's fantastic. We used to go all the time, but I haven't been in a while. It's the perfect student place. Huge portions, homey atmosphere, cheap."

When we pulled up in front, he turned to me. "Wait for me, okay? I want to make sure you don't fall out of the truck or slip."

I nodded. I hated feeling helpless, but he'd seen me struggle to get in, and my heeled boots were not the best on the ice.

He came around and opened the cab door, filling the doorway and lifting his hands up to me. I could tell he wanted to lift me down with his hands on my waist, but I put my gloved hands in his instead. He gave me a little huff of disapproval, but let me jump myself down using his hands without any comment.

I took one step onto the slick sidewalk and almost fell, clutching at Aaron's sleeve to balance myself. He immediately reacted, steady in his grippy boots, taking hold of my hand and tucking it into the crook of his arm. I smiled up at him gratefully and clung to him tightly as I picked my way across the ice to the door of the restaurant.

We were swiftly seated at a table, waters poured, specials rattled off with an efficiency that said they did brisk business all lunch hour. It was just barely noon and already three-quarters full, tables around us buzzing pleasantly.

"What are you having?" He was studying his menu intently, in between quick glances at me.

I hid my smugness at the effect my sweater was having but had to laugh at the sight of him, nose in the menu like always. It was time to put on my investigator's hat.

"Has the menu changed much since you last came?" I put on a straight face when he looked up at my laugh.

"No."

"Do you remember it well?"

"Yes." He didn't understand what I was getting at.

"Do you know what you're having?"

"Of course. What's up?"

I shook my head at him, still smiling. "Why do you need to read the whole menu if you know it by heart and you know exactly what you're having?"

"Oh." He was sheepish now. "I don't know. I just like to read all the descriptions and see if there are any changes, I guess. I have my favorites, but I always go through it again, just in case."

I hadn't meant to embarrass him. I moved on. "I think I've decided on the lunch lasagna, if you're ready?"

He got the chicken cacciatore and a side salad. The server brought his salad out to start. I goggled at it. The side portion was a full dinner plate piled high. Aaron grinned at me, one and a half dimples peeking out next to his beard. His grin was spectacular.

"Now you see why we came here so much. You can always count on being well-fed at Cordera's." He gave a big thumbs-up like he was in a cheesy commercial, and I laughed again.

He let me steal a few bites and black olives off his giant plate while I waited for my food. It was companionable to eat together, to look at other people's orders and speculate about what they got, to chat about nothing in particular.

I told him about the Halloween events the various colleges and student associations had been putting on. I wasn't involved in planning any of them, but I was tracking them in the events calendar I compiled. My plan for Halloween was to stay home and hand out candy. Aaron had promised to go trick or treating with his nephews. He was picking them up early and taking them around to the farms in the area.

"Send me pictures. I bet they'll be adorable."

"Definitely will." He kept plowing through his salad but looked very pleased I had asked. When our food came, he handed the giant salad plate back to the server to make more room on our table. He'd made a considerable dent in it.

"You must get hungry with all the work you do." I eyed him, alarmed, as he dug into his pasta like it was his last meal. "What on earth are your grocery bills like?"

"You don't want to know, trust me. Every day I have a pre-breakfast protein shake, breakfast, snack, lunch, snack, supper, snack. I eat like a hobbit. I've considered buying stocks in protein bars. Nothing keeps me going like them for a quick afternoon break."

I pictured him, covered in dust, holding a bar that tasted like chalk in one hand, eating standing up, barely taking the time to stop, and suddenly wanted to take care of him. Why did I want to fuss over him, when he so clearly had his life figured out better than I did?

"So why did you have the extra time for lunch today? Do things slow down in the fall and winter?" I took another molten bite of lasagna. It was so hot that I had to cut small bites and let each one cool on my fork.

"In the winter, yes, but we have lots of indoor work we can do. Basements, stuff like that."

"Do you take a break over Christmas?" It's not what I really wanted to know, but it was close. I was suddenly desperate to know what he did for the holidays. I was an orphan child in a cheesy movie, pressed up against the window, watching a picture-perfect family exchanging presents around a tree.

"Yeah, of course. We block off three weeks, and I give the guys paid time off to make up for summer being nonstop." He gestured with his fork. Most of his cacciatore was already gone. "Do you get a break in December?"

"Oh, the campus basically shuts down after the fifteenth. I think we'll be all cleaned up by the next day, and we won't be back till after the New Year. I'll probably work ahead from home."

"You're not flying east to see your aunt?"

"I would consider it, but she's going to Mexico with her friends over Christmas. I think I'll just be cozy at home. I'm already stocking up on wine and candles, and I bought some twinkly lights the other day. I'll hang them next week, maybe." My place would look adorable with lights in the living room and around my kitchen cabinets.

I smiled just thinking about it, and he smiled back, but had a look in his eye I couldn't parse. Maybe my cozy plans seemed pathetic compared to his bigger family gatherings.

"Do you miss your mom on the holidays?" He asked it softly, perhaps offering me a chance to pretend not to hear him.

"Yes," I said simply. His eyes were so patient on mine that I went on. "We never had much at the holidays when she was sick, but she always cooked something special, and Aunt Bea decorated our tiny plastic tree with tinsel. It wasn't elaborate, but I think we did okay."

Aaron settled up with our server, waving away my mild protest that I could get my own meal. I'd come to learn that this group of friends was generous that way, buying each other rounds, picking up tabs, and bringing each other little gifts at random. Maybe I'd pick up his tab at our next pub night.

He stood up and picked up the jacket draped over the back of his chair, eyeing me as I got up and shimmied my skirt smoothly over my thighs before getting my coat. My short swingy bob was the perfect length for this season, letting me wrap my scarf without it getting in the way. I followed him out to the truck, and he stopped me at the passenger door with a raised hand.

"Why don't you let me lift you in this time? That skirt is not compatible with climbing."

I eyed each of his arms pointedly, coyly. "How much do you bench?"

His whole face came alight with challenge. "Don't worry about it. I lift for a living."

He paused, maybe waiting for me to argue, but I just turned around to face the door, curious what he would do. His hands came firmly around my waist, digging in as he lifted me straight up. I caught the grip and stepped in, conscious of him close behind me, crowding me to keep me steady. My ass brushed up against his chest, and my breath caught. Once he saw I was settled. he came around to his side.

"Now, that was easier, wasn't it?" He made his ruling calmly, as though he hadn't had a face full of my ass.

"Was it? What about for my pride?" It was worth it to get his hands on me.

"Well, that's the sacrifice we make for that killer skirt. I don't mind sacrificing if you don't." He grinned devastatingly at me, and I felt like I'd dropped into a new dimension. I needed to level up to match this open, comfortable flirting somehow. He was outpacing me at every turn.

"Hmm," was all I could muster. "If you like it so much, I'll try to bear the humiliation."

"Thank you, that's very kind of you."

When he dropped me off, he came around again to help me down, and this time I let him take me around the waist again and slide me down close to his body. I gripped his biceps, but his coat was too bulky for me to feel them flexed under my hands. His face was tipped toward mine, watching me. I had to tamp down the urge to lift my arms around his neck or raise my face for a kiss. This was not a date, even if it felt like one. And it was the middle of the day, and we were outside my office. I ran through those three points twice before I could step away from him.

"Thanks for lunch, Aaron. See you again!" I was almost at the building as I spoke, hurrying away before the magnetic pull of him drew me back in.

"Bye, Evelyn. You can wear that skirt again if you want. I don't mind helping you into my truck."

Cheeky. I heard him laughing as I stuck up the middle finger of my gloved hand and practically ran inside.

Chapter Nine

❧

I checked my phone and groaned. Aaron was texting me, as he had been off and on since last week's lunch. It was both comforting and alarming to see his name on my screen. He had been in my living room, he'd been in my office, and now he was on the phone in my bedroom. He was mounting a stealth assault, a siege, slowly surrounding my castle, with all the tools he needed to cross the moat, avoid the boiling oil, and outsmart my archers.

If I was truthful, I'd admit my defenders were sleeping on the job. Someone had left the drawbridge down and the portcullis up. He was all but invited to waltz right in.

You want a ride?

Another notification chimed.

I'm heading over to the pub in 20. I can swing by for you

It was nice of him to offer, but I was not leaving my couch for any reason. I had got my period late last night, and all I had done all day was watch the full 1995 *Pride and Prejudice*. After over five hours of Austen, dozing and highly medicated, all I was capable of was reheating my wheat bag in the microwave and maybe scrounging for food. The first day was always the worst. If it happened to fall on a weekend, I took full advantage of not having to work through my cramps and stayed in a nest all day long.

But I had to tell Aaron something. I'd already texted Grace, but I never thought he'd threaten to come get me. I would have to text him, and then I could reheat my bag and maybe start *Persuasion*. Or *Mansfield Park*. May as well go full Austen. I wondered how Lizzy Bennet dealt with her period. She probably just walked it off.

Sorry, not feeling great…

I started, and then stopped. If I carried on that way, he'd ask me what was wrong or offer to take me to the doctor or something. And then I'd have to explain. I may as well be up-front from the start. As he was an actual adult, he should be able to handle it.

I backspaced and started over.

Got my period. Cramps. Miserable. Not going out tonight. But thx for the offer.

There, that should shut down anything further. He texted back almost right away.

Poor Ev.

Can I come and bring you dinner? I'll pick whatever you want. You can kick me out whenever you want, even right away.

I hadn't had time to buy groceries during the week, and I had no energy to make food. There weren't even chips in my cupboard. Or chocolate. Suddenly I needed a burger and fries like my next breath.

I wanted to see Aaron. I wanted food to come to my door. It would be the ideal solution, if I wasn't still in pj's, unshowered. I didn't even remember brushing my teeth that morning. I picked up my phone again to respond.

Cheeseburger. No onions, unless they're caramelized. Everything else, yes.

Fries. Sweet potato fries even better

I considered my apartment and my appearance another moment.

If you get here before 7:30, I won't let you in

He must have been waiting by the phone, his response came so fast.

See you at 7:31.

I showered but didn't wash my hair. I could not be bothered to dry it. A headband would have to do. I considered my clothes. There was no way I was going with tight or seductive today. Aaron would have to be happy with loungewear Evie again. Yoga pants—my softest and most stretchy—and another very comfortable bralette, my black one this time, with a slouchy necked sweater that enveloped me like a hug.

I felt so much better after my hot shower and changing my clothes, and I had a little zip from waiting for Aaron. It even made a dent in how bloated and crampy I felt. A small dent. I looked around the room and decided not to clean up. It was my rest day, and he could take my place as it was.

At seven twenty-seven, I saw his shadow against the outdoor light. True to his word, he didn't knock until seven thirty-one. I opened the door for him and he came in with hands full of bags.

"Hi." I took in his stuff, bewildered. How much had he bought?

He smiled a hello and handed me a paper bag. "Here's your burger. Why don't you get comfortable and start eating?"

It smelled so good I didn't object. Maybe he had done some grocery shopping while he was out and didn't want his produce to freeze in the truck.

He came in and paused in the living room doorway, taking me in, his eyes flitting and cataloging. I was already deep in my blanket nest, burger in hand. I took him in too. He looked like a feather bed I could sink into. He was wearing dark gray sweatpants and a faded blue t-shirt that draped over his torso and strained over his shoulders. His arms were thick all the way up. He was thick all over, strong and muscled, but cushioned by a soft layer—an appealing combination of hard and soft, comforting and overwhelming.

He had a burger bag of his own in one hand and a grocery bag in the other. He set it down on the coffee table and started unpacking it.

"I put some ice cream in your freezer. I wasn't sure what kind to get, so I got a few different little ones. Vanilla, chocolate fudge, and a chocolate chip cookie dough. If you hate one of those, I can take it home instead."

I shook my head at him. "You didn't have to do that."

"I know, but I know what cramps can be like. Alice was always in a lot of pain when we were younger. I wanted to do something for you."

Alice was his sister, I remembered. His gaze was soft and concerned, one brow up as if to ask if it was okay that he was there, intruding further into my life, trying to take care of me. I didn't have an answer for that brow. I took another fry to avoid responding.

He turned back to his grocery bag. "I got chocolate—dark and milk, just in case. And chips and dip, chocolate chip cookies, bananas, and chamomile tea." He trailed off, his face turning sheepish and shy.

He was now speaking almost under his breath. I had to strain to hear him. "I read that bananas and chamomile tea are both good for cramps. You don't have to have any of it if you don't want."

"And I got this." He pulled out a tiny rosebush in a little pot. It had pinkish-red buds all over, and one full bloom. He had a similar color in his cheeks as he held it out toward me. "I thought you might like it."

The rosebuds were nearly the exact color of the bra he'd admired at length. I bit the corners of my lip to keep from smiling smugly.

His voice took on a defensive tone, though I still hadn't said anything. "It was near the bananas. They had a display of plants."

I had to stop him before he worked himself up into real embarrassment. "It's beautiful. Thank you for everything. It's the perfect care package." I smiled at him before fishing another fry out of the greasy paper bag. He put my rose plant in the middle of my coffee table and turned it so the open bloom faced me, making my smile bigger yet.

He picked up his paper bag again. "So, can I stay and have a burger with you? Or would you rather be left alone?"

"Stay. Please."

He grinned at me and got busy opening his burger, and squeezed onto the couch next to me, a delicious furnace all along one side of my body. I didn't move over to give him even an inch more room.

He motioned at the TV, the menu for *Pride and Prejudice* still on the screen. "What are we watching?"

"I finished *Pride and Prejudice*, but I was thinking of starting another Austen. Do you want to watch *Persuasion*?"

He didn't hesitate. "Sure. I'll watch anything."

We watched the movie on the couch together,

pausing to make tea or get ice cream. Aaron occasionally asked questions like how the Musgroves were related to Anne or which captain was which. I liked seeing him so invested in Anne's quietly passionate love story. My cramps faded to a dull ache in the background, and I barely noticed them for the first time all day.

At the end of the movie, when Anne and her captain were reunited at last, I realized that Aaron and I had become completely intertwined, so naturally and gradually I had barely noticed. We had started the movie with his arm draped over my shoulder, heavy and comforting like a weighted blanket. After we paused for ice cream, the blankets got wrapped around both of us, him joining me in my nest like he belonged there.

Now, I was fully on top of him, sitting sideways in his lap, with my cheek to his chest and his chin on the top of my head. He had one hand firmly under my knee, holding my curled-up legs. His other hand was on the back of my neck, massaging gently, one thick finger down the neck of my shirt, sliding under my bralette to play with the lace strap.

I was in bliss. His shirt felt like the softest cashmere, it was so well-worn. I realized I had his massive shoulder in one hand and was flexing my fingers in his shirt like a cat. I felt close to purring too. I turned my face into his chest and rubbed my achy eyes on his soft shirt.

He spoke, and I felt his voice rumble through me, vibrating out through his chest. "We should get you to bed, sleepy."

"Don't wanna," I mumbled back, speaking directly into his pecs. "Too comfy."

His hand moved from my leg and came up to my chin, tilting me back to look up at him. We stared at each other at point-blank range. I wondered idly if I could seduce him into cuddling with me all night as my own personal, full-body hot water bottle.

His mouth drifted down toward mine as I stared up at him, leisurely, slowly, his hand firm on the back of my head. The hand that had lifted my face trailed down the front of my neck and settled lightly at the base of my throat, making me shiver. He had me surrounded. He moved carefully, eyebrows lowered and intense, both holding me firm and giving me a chance to pull away. A breath away, he paused, waiting. Waiting for me to close the gap.

I broke free and stood up. His arms fell away at the first sign I was pulling away, and his head leaned back. He closed his eyes, the picture of embarrassment and frustration. He looked delicious. He gripped the back of the couch with one hand, took a deep breath, and opened his eyes. I could tell he was about to apologize.

I shushed him with one hand on his shoulder and crawled awkwardly back over his lap to straddle him.

"I'm coming back. I just didn't want to crane my neck."

His breath gusted out and his hands came to my thighs, pulling me higher up and closer to his full mouth. His fingers dug in. I could detect the tremor running up his arms as I trailed my hands up them and wound them around his neck. He was tense and ready, waiting. Waiting for me.

I leaned forward and closed the gap between us, sealing our mouths together softly. The tension in him snapped into movement, his arms coming around my body in a bear hug, squeezing. One hand traveled up my back to cradle my head again, the other traveled down to press my lower body closer to his. He sighed contentedly into the kiss. I smiled against his lips, only to sigh myself when he changed the angle of the kiss and deepened the pressure of his mouth on mine, his hand tangling in my hair.

We communicated in groans and sighs, in squeezes and subtle shifts, with tongues and teeth. It was our best talk yet.

I was on fire. No amount of contact would be enough. I pressed closer, flattening my chest against his, giving in to my need for deep pressure. My tongue was inside his mouth now, exploring and stroking, and he was groaning and holding on to my hip, his thumb wrapped around the front of my hip bone, digging in. He slowly ground his hips up into me as if he couldn't help himself. He was hard and thick against my belly, making me ache.

I wanted to strip us both down and taste him all over. His warm citrus scent surrounded me, making me dizzy. I was all sensation and lit-up nerves, overwhelmed by how he surrounded me on all sides but still laser-focused on his mouth and the way it gave and firmed under mine. My hands held his head in a firm grip, and he let me lead the way, nipping and testing, exploring as I pleased. Mine to conquer.

Both of his hands were on my ass now, one meaty hand on each cheek, fingertips digging in toward the centerline. I wanted them imprinted so deep I'd feel it in the morning. It felt amazing. Then he pulled me higher and lined me up against him, pressing exactly where I ached the most. I gasped for a breath. We had gone from sleepy cuddling to inferno so fast I had whiplash.

Before I realized it, my hands were on his pecs, pushing back in a universal "Stop" signal. He froze.

"Ev." His voice was a rasp. He sounded like he needed some air. He sounded like he didn't care if he ever breathed a full breath again. "You okay?" His hands were still on my ass, firm, but not pressing, giving me an anchor.

"Yeah." I was panting like I'd been sprinting. "Just, you know, trying to catch up. This is going fast."

His eyes searched my face, dark in the low light from the TV. "We can stop any time." One heavy hand gently trailed up my spine. "I love seeing you worked up like this." He surveyed my flushed face and my still-parted mouth like he'd been the one conquering. Smug and satisfied, almost a smirk.

He lowered his voice to almost a whisper, but that rough rasp remained. "You're so fucking gorgeous, Ev."

A shiver ran all the way down my spine at the look in his eyes. His hands tightened again on me, and he looked at me even more intently. His mouth was red and still wet, the indents from my teeth marking his full bottom lip. I wanted those lips and the rasp of his beard all over me. I wanted to hear exactly what he wanted to do to me.

I couldn't handle all the desire rising like panic in my chest. Longing and wanting settled in constraining bands around me, making my heart race in an entirely new way. I had to move.

He didn't miss the change on my face or the way I was suddenly tense as a rock on top of him.

"Okay?" he asked softly. At my stiff nod, he went back to the bear hug, soothing me down onto his chest, my head on his shoulder, hands stroking deep and smooth up and down my back. His erection was a bar underneath me, but he seemed ready to ignore it.

He heaved a sigh that trailed into a hum, sending gentle vibrations through me again. "It's okay. Just relax. When you're ready, I'll tell you what else I think about you. Not to mention everything I've thought about doing to you."

He paused at my sharp inhale. "Wait, that's maybe too intense. Forget all that for now. I'm just your friendly neighborhood Aaron who's always semi-hard for you."

He chuckled then as I laughed into his shoulder helplessly, hands still soothing on my back. "No, wait, that's too much too. Just a guy you know who's ready to blow all over your couch." I was hiccupping now, and he took pity on me, reaching over to pick up my mug of now-cool chamomile.

I pushed off his shoulder to sip it, enjoying his eyes on me. The way they roved over my face and down, lingering on my breasts and taking in the sight of me straddling him made me feel beautiful and sensual, like he was hungrily memorizing me forever in his mind. If I could stroll down his mental portrait gallery, maybe I'd see this moment framed in gold and hung in a place of honor.

He seemed to be thinking along the same lines. "Let's do this again, exactly. Except naked, next time."

I snorted into my tea, one hand still on his shoulder for balance. His hands were wrapped on my thighs now, gentle, but like he couldn't stand not touching me for even a moment.

I smiled wryly at him. "Sorry for freaking out." He shook his head at my words, but I continued. "I was having a very good time. I just got too in my head about it. Maybe we should call it a night."

I felt wiped out all of a sudden. The ache in my low back had returned, and I was bloated and heavy again. My brain and body were both getting in the way of having any more fun today.

"Ev, I'm just here to make you happy tonight. Don't worry about it." He smiled and squeezed my thighs once. The corner of his mouth slanted up, and I knew he was going to tease me again. "But if at some point it makes you happy to get on your knees in front of me, I'll gladly let you do that."

This one sounded straight out of his fantasies. I had a momentary mental picture of crawling on my knees to help him out of his sweatpants and showing him exactly what I could do with my mouth. It was so tempting that if I had been feeling better, I might have.

He interrupted my sexual imaginings by taking the mug out of my hand. It had tilted dangerously while I was in dreamland. He put it down on the table and wrapped his hand around my neck again, pulling me down to his mouth. It was a goodbye kiss, a soft coda to our evening, soothing and gentle and over too soon.

"Go get ready for bed. I'll clean up and then head out." He slapped my ass in a friendly way, and I rose, dismissed, from his lap.

I went and washed my face, dealt with the rest of me, and cursed my period. I could have been having sex already. I changed into my pj top and a pair of shorts, leaving my soft bralette on for some containment. I wasn't willing to free-boob around Aaron yet.

I glared at my reflection in the mirror as I brushed my teeth, trying to will myself into some gumption. Was I never going to just ask for what I wanted?

I nearly marched back to the kitchen where he was rinsing the last ice cream spoon and putting it in my dish rack. Such a polite, helpful man. I no longer thought his big shoulders overwhelmed my cozy kitchen. He fit right in.

I straightened my shoulders. "Will you stay with me, just for an hour? I'm feeling kind of pathetic, and you're so warm and comfortable…" I trailed off but rallied with another burst of honesty. "It makes me feel better when you hold me."

There. I'd said something.

He turned, wiping his hands on a kitchen towel. "I thought you'd never ask." He paused, obviously calculating. "If I let myself out later, how will I lock the door?"

"The bolt is one of those old-school ones with the knob. It'll lock behind you."

He walked over to examine it, shaking his head when it didn't pass muster. "You really should get a proper deadbolt. They're much more secure."

"I'll keep it in mind to mention to the landlady. Now, are you coming with me?" I held out a hand for him. He took it and followed me down the short hallway and into the bedroom.

He was in my bedroom. Now he truly had invaded everywhere. He'd grown again somehow, crowding the room. He looked around with obvious interest, cataloging my possessions, even letting go of my hand to pick up my candle and smell it. He'd be trying my perfume next.

I bent over and threw back the covers and felt his gaze settle on me again with a satisfying weight. He watched me crawl under the blankets, unable to contain his grin, and turned off the lamp for me, climbing in after me.

His arm tucked under my head as though we'd been sleeping together forever, and my hand found his on the pillow. He tugged my hips back until I was snugged up against him, his pelvis flush against my bottom, the backs of my thighs glued to the front of his. His chest pressed against my back and his arm came around my waist, looking for my other hand. I could have felt self-conscious that he was touching my round belly, but he was such a comforting weight that I didn't care. I twined my fingers with his, and we lay together without saying a word. His face brushed back and forth lightly in my hair, breathing me in.

I could feel my arousal keying up, picturing his hands on my breasts, feeling him hard behind me. But his overwhelming heat sank deep into the tension in my back, and all my muscles went loose. I was swept into sleep with the comfort of him surrounding me, not feeling when he left, not waking until the sun was in my eyes the next morning.

Chapter Ten

✦❧✦

Sunday morning was leached of color, the November sky a pale, watery blue, the sunlight frosty and insipid. How could such a cloudless day seem so dreary? A thin, fresh layer of snow on the ground reflected back the same pale, colorless light.

I puttered around my apartment, alone. I cleaned, did yoga, made a grocery list and a meal plan for the week. My calendar and emails were up to date. It was all very productive, and I should have felt satisfied.

Instead, I checked my phone every other minute. There had been a text from Aaron late the night before, around two-thirty a.m. He must have sent it from his truck as he left. It was a simple "I hope I didn't wake you. Thanks for letting me stay tonight." And that was it. Nothing since.

It was three p.m., and I was thinking of delaying the grocery shop I desperately needed and opening a bottle of wine instead, which was a great solution to being restless and lonely while on pain meds. I should just call him, right? Or text him. I had responded with a quick "I'm glad you came over. You should market yourself as a sleep aid because I slept great" and hoped that it struck the appropriate tone. The problem was I didn't know what tone to strike. Flirty? Cool and casual? I had never overthought a text like this in my life.

My phone rang, interrupting my spiral. I checked the screen, caught between hope and anxiety. It was Grace. My heart sank and lifted at the same time. I couldn't handle this rollercoaster anymore. I wanted to reclaim my quiet life.

"Hello?"

"Evie!" She was practically screaming into the phone. "What happened last night? Why haven't you texted me? *Tell me everything*."

"I..."

She interrupted me before I could finish. "Wait. I have to come over. Tell me I can come over. Are you busy now?"

I had to laugh. "I was about to go out for groceries. I need to get a few things for the week. It's going to be crazy busy. There's something like ten major events on campus this week."

"Shit, that's right. Why don't I come pick you up? Shopping is better with a car anyway. We can catch up and get both our groceries done, and then I have to get ready for dinner with my dad."

"Sure, sounds great. When should I be ready?"

"I'll be there in twenty." She hung up, and I went to finish my grocery list and gather my shopping bags.

We caught up as we walked companionably through the aisles together. I was going to take advantage of having a car and stock up my pantry so I could get a bunch of cooking done for the week. I would need to pack lunch and supper most days since I'd be hosting some of the evening events.

Grace put her basket in the top section of my cart. "Ugh, these cans are getting heavy."

I looked down at my chest. "Tell me about it," I said wryly. She followed my gaze down, and we both started cackling like hyenas in the spice aisle.

After she wiped her eyes, she pointed at me. "I've been very patient, but now it's time to spill. Your list is almost done, and we're running out of time."

"What do you want to know?"

"Oh, I don't know, *everything*? You texted me that you weren't coming, and then about an hour later

Aaron texted that he wasn't going to make it. He rarely misses pub nights. I was suspicious. So then I texted him back like, 'Hope Evie is ok.' And he texted me back a little later with 'She's doing fine, I'm at her place now.' And I of course refrained from sending anything else because I am very cool, but I wanted to text you ten exclamation points."

"You sneaky bastard."

"I take that as a compliment."

"Fine. He came over. He brought me a burger, and tea, and chocolate, and ice cream. And chips! He literally thought of everything someone who's menstruating would want. Grace, I swear to you that he did *research* on what helps period cramps."

"Well. Isn't he smooth. A regular knight in shining armor." She pursed full lips. "Aaron to the rescue."

I didn't understand her tone. "I know, right? And then we watched *Persuasion,* and he was actually interested. And we cuddled during the movie. And he rubbed my neck." I paused and then said the rest in a rush. "And-then-we-made-out-but-I-freaked-out-a-bit-and-kicked-him-out-but-reconsidered-and-I-invited-him-to-bed-to-hold-me-and-he-left-at-three."

"WHAT?" Grace exploded, ignoring a shopper at the end of the aisle that was giving us the eye. "You made out? You freaked out? You kicked him out? You slept together?"

"That was a very good summation of the evening. You should be a journalist."

She shook her head at me, her swaying head wrap underlining her point. "Don't distract me with compliments. Tell me about this make-out. Was it good? Are you going to do it again?"

I groaned. "He's so sexy I can't even handle it. Why does he have to be so good at kissing? And talking? And with his hands?" I trailed off. "His hands. I'm developing an addiction. It's a problem."

Grace gaped at me. "Holy shit. You have it bad." She held up a finger to stop my protests and used it to emphasize every word. "When are you going to hop on that dick?" She shuddered and gagged. "Ew. I've never said that about Aaron. It feels wrong."

I groaned again and hid my face in my arms, resting on top of my grocery cart. "Grace." My voice was muffled. "Don't torture me. I don't know what to do with him."

I heard her snort from somewhere above me, but her hand on my shoulder rubbed a comforting circle. "I mean, he probably has some ideas if you don't know what to do. I've seen him eyeing you."

I stood and looked at her. "He's got ideas. But, uh...If I do happen to go a few rounds with him, will it make things weird with everyone else?"

Her tone was soothing, like I was a cranky

toddler. I was probably not far off, actually. "It'll be fine. Don't worry about it. We might be a little overexcited at first, but we'll calm down eventually. And hey, despite how we're acting right now, we're all adults. We'll let you two sort it out. Just go with your gut for now."

It was good advice. I couldn't help but remember the mysterious Chris and his ex, though. That was a breakup that hadn't gone well. But on the other hand, Lucy and Aaron had dated, and they were still friends.

This is why casual hookups were easier.

I flashed back to last night on my couch with Aaron, the pull between us so strong it had nearly towed me under. The memory of the heat we'd generated put burning spots in my cheeks. My last casual hookup had been nothing like that. The man with the shiny veneers kept clinking our teeth together as we kissed, and I couldn't even remember if I'd come after his fumbling efforts.

Casual hookups did have their downsides.

Grace and I finished up our respective lists in silence and checked out. She put a box of condoms in my cart at the last minute and stared me down until I gave in and paid for them.

"When will you see each other next, do you

think?" Grace asked, putting her groceries beside mine in the trunk of the car.

"I don't know. I thought I might hear from him today, but he hasn't texted at all. My week is busy." I shrugged, trying not to care.

"I think he usually does a day at the farm on Sundays. He's probably buried under nephews and showing them how to drive snowmobiles or something equally dangerous." Grace looked at me, all sympathy. "I'm sure he'll text soon."

We exchanged hugs at my place, and Grace threatened me on pain of death if I didn't keep her updated. "I'm not going to lie, it's strange for me. But I'll try not to be weirded out. Just don't tell me too many details, please."

A FEW HOURS LATER I WAS MAKING A CHICKPEA curry and a big pot of rice for my suppers when my phone chimed from the living room where it was charging. I had to check it to see if it was Aaron, but I didn't want to burn my garlic. I considered giving him his own tone, so I would know right away.

Soon enough the tomatoes were in, simmering away, and I could check my phone.

It *was* Aaron. Warmth rose in my chest at his

name. It disturbed me. Maybe it was heartburn, but it felt a lot like happiness.

Hi, how was your day? I'm heading home from my parents. I wish I could see you today, but I have to finish payroll or no one will want to work for me anymore. Call you later? Catch up? Phone sex?

I smiled at the block of text. And the hopeful question at the end, probably part joke, part serious question. I was starting to get used to it, the gift of his thoughts stated plainly, openly. It made me want to gift him mine back, wrap them in a little bow, and let him unravel me at will.

Drive safe, okay? Don't text me if you're on the road. If you're good and finish your work, you can call me later

Was I going to address the phone sex?

If you're very good, maybe I'll get out my vibrator

There, that was the closest I'd ever gotten to a sext. I didn't usually masturbate on my period, but before yesterday I wouldn't have thought anyone would be able to make me almost forget about first-day cramps. With Aaron, it seemed, anything was possible.

After supper, I settled into the couch, back in my nest, watching whatever videos the algorithm suggested for me—cooking, art, movie reviews, cosplay artists, any low-stakes distraction.

Halfway through an artist's process video, the phone rang. I jumped at it.

"Hello?"

"Hi, are you free, or should I call later?" His voice was deep and smooth tonight, unlike the rasp he'd had yesterday when he was hard beneath me. I flashed warm all over at the memory.

"I'm not doing anything much. But I was thinking of getting ready for bed." There, that sounded normal enough.

"I can call back if you want? Then you won't have to think about it."

We hung up, and I quickly brushed my teeth and did my skincare. I had only been sitting on my bed a minute when he called again. I was craving the solid weight of him. He'd thoroughly staked his claim on my bed already. With a pillow hugged to my chest, I wished he was there to wrap himself around me while I told him about my lackluster day. His voice in my ear made it seem like he could be behind me, whispering into it.

"So, how was your day?" I had to get a grip.

"It was good, but long. There are always chores to

do at the farm. Chris called on my way home, so I swung by to help him with a sagging front step. I'll have to finish up payroll tomorrow first thing."

"An extra-early start? What happened to your vaunted work-life boundaries? A little birdie told me they were set in stone."

"Friends and family always come first. And my work crew. I answer the phone for them. Clients, I try to keep within business hours."

"Ah, I see. Well, it's good that you take care of your crew. Have you decided on employee gifts?"

He sighed, ending in a deep grumble. "Not yet. I can't do booze because I have a recovering alcoholic on the crew. I've done cash in the past, so maybe that's still the best way to go. Everyone likes a little extra cash at the holidays."

He'd been procrastinating, I could tell. How nice to know he didn't have all the answers, all the time.

"Cash is good. But cash handed out at a work dinner would make it more special. Have you ever done something at the pub? You could make it come-and-go, invite partners, pick up the tab. Pool and darts are right there for people to entertain themselves."

"That's a good idea. Some of the guys hang out, and I'm sure they'd love the chance to beat me at darts."

I could hear him rustling around in the background.

"Hang on, I'm just writing this down. I'll email the owner to book it after I'm done talking to you."

"Wow, you waste no time." I'd never worked with a single client who went from suggestion to ready to book their event within a minute.

"No sense in waffling. The idea is good. If it sucks, I can do something different next year."

I blinked. Just like that, he had made a decision and had a game plan and even a plan to evaluate it afterward for future years. Standard event planning procedure. He kept surprising me.

"Well, you can put me on retainer if you need any other ideas for gifts or parties. As long as this is the most work I have to do for it."

He chuckled. "Send me your rates. You're hired. I do need to buy something for my nephews. It's gotta be dinosaurs for Brandon and comic books for Jace."

"How old?" I pictured little brown-haired Aaron copies, delight on their faces, fingers tearing into wrapping paper.

"Six and nine. They're still pretty easy to buy for. Alice always sends a detailed list."

"Do you get her something too?"

"This year, yes. Last year I had Rob, my brother-in-law. I got him a gift card for tools and a bottle of

Crown Royal. Alice sent me her list at the beginning of October. With links."

I smiled even though he couldn't see me. "I love an organized woman."

"Yeah, she'd like you too. She can be pretty forceful, so I bet you'd find a clashing point if you spent a lot of time together."

If Aaron, Mr. Magistrate, was calling her forceful, she must be an opinion tornado. I gulped at the idea of spending enough time with his sister to rub each other the wrong way. I hadn't pictured myself sitting by a crackling fire and surrounded by boisterous children and opinionated family members. I still had my mittens pressed up against the windows in my mind.

"What about you?" Aaron interrupted my minispiral. "Are you doing gifts? Sending something to your aunt?"

"I'll send her gift cards. She'll probably buy herself books and send me a picture. I thought about sending her a package, but she's so frugal, she'll hate if I waste money on shipping. I will probably send her something extra so she can buy herself treats when she flies. I have ideas for Joel and Grace, but do they usually do gifts?"

"It's hit-or-miss. Sometimes we've done a white elephant thing where everyone brings something small. It depends on the year, on who's around. Joel and Douglas often fly west to visit family. Actually, I'm the only one without family all over the country."

I liked giving gifts, but I didn't want to be the one who made everyone feel bad if I showed up with a bunch of presents. Maybe I would give Grace, Joel, and Melanie something on our last day at the office. And Aaron. Should I get him something? Lucy? Douglas? Suddenly the whole season was fraught with danger to tiptoe through. This had never been a problem before.

"What's on your list?" I was curious what kind of things he asked for.

"Well, I usually ask my family for gift cards to hardware stores, since I always have a tool I need to replace."

"You ask for work stuff?" I must have sounded disappointed because he laughed.

"Don't worry, they ignore me. They get me coffee, alcohol, socks, kitchen stuff that my sister thinks I need, like an immersion blender, and my mom always gets me pajamas, even though I'm a grown man and haven't worn a matching pair of pj's since I was 12. She also gets me underwear. Which is fine, but I am perfectly capable of buying my own."

I snorted. He sounded so aggrieved. "What's wrong with matching pj's?"

"They never fit properly. And they're too warm to

sleep in. Plus, there's only so much plaid I want in my life. But I use my immersion blender a lot, and the underwear *does* fit perfectly, so I can't complain too much."

I laughed. "Poor man, so well cared for by his family. Must be a hardship."

"Yeah, yeah, I know I've got it pretty good."

"You can say that again."

He paused. "So, when are you going to invite me over again?"

"You mean, when are you going to invite yourself over?"

"Yes, exactly," he answered without hesitation.

I had to laugh. He was shameless. "I won't have time this week. I'm hosting three evening events and on call for others. But I'm not hosting the one on Saturday, so I'll see you at the pub."

He seemed to consider. "And can I pick you up and drive you home after?"

"Yes. You can even come over after."

"Why don't I come over before, and we can skip the pub altogether?"

"No, I want to see everyone. Especially since I missed last night."

"Okay. I'll wait. But I might call you again this week. I might not be able to resist."

"Have you ever considered playing it cooler?" I had to ask.

"I did play it cool, for like a month. I've decided to go full burners now." He had been playing it cool? I shook my head. Surely there had to be a middle gear.

"I should let you go." My yawn cut off my sentence, perfectly timed.

"Okay, sleepy," he said in a teasing tone. "We'll save the phone sex for another night. Just know that I will be jacking off in about ten minutes." He continued like he hadn't said anything unusual. "I'll text you tomorrow."

Holy shit. How did I go from yawning to squirming so quickly? The whiplash I felt around him —first lulled into cozy surrender and then suddenly worked up and desperate for more. I couldn't quite imagine myself putting on a throaty voice and mustering up dirty talk for him. But he made me want to try, to be adventurous, to put myself out there.

The silence stretched. "Did I scare you off?" He was a quiet rumble again. "I like teasing you, but I don't want to freak you out."

"No. Just wondering what to do about you."

"You don't have to do anything. Don't worry about it." His voice was deeper now, and warm, but he didn't sound embarrassed. "I'm going to hang up now, before I get into trouble. Goodnight, Evie."

My phone now turned off, I settled back, still wondering what to do about him. Fucking around in my new friend group seemed inadvisable, but I already knew it wasn't going to stop me. Lust had me deep within its clawed grip. I'd just let him bang himself right out of my system. That had always worked in the past. I paused, trying to remember a time where I'd wanted someone specific rather than just an attractive and willing person to help slake my momentary thirst. Surely there had been someone.

There was definitely someone. I would think of him any minute.

Aaron's expressive eyebrows popped into my head, one side lifting skeptically. I answered them in my mind. *You're not that special.* Both raised now. *Okay, maybe a little special.* One deep dimple joined the eyebrows in my mind, smugly contented with my concession. Always had to get the last word.

Chapter Eleven

✦

The week was both a slog and a blur. Blake Smith from the music department called me every fifteen minutes with yet another problem with their winter music program. Volunteer ushers dropped out, the choirs had different length sets, they couldn't get eggnog in the right quantity, they didn't have a way to keep the cider warm, there weren't enough chairs for the cellists.

All problems that he could have solved but instead came with hands wringing to me. So I rounded up volunteers, asked emcees to pad out the time between choirs, ordered more cider to compensate for the eggnog, borrowed extra plug-in carafes from another department, requisitioned more chairs, and solved every other little problem.

Joel lectured me whenever he heard me on another call with Blake. "What happened to training them to figure this shit out on their own? You're a resource, but it's their event, and they should be responsible for it."

I didn't have time for his lectures. "It's faster to do it myself. There's only so many times I can listen to a grown adult call in tears." I paused as I was about to make yet another phone call. "I still don't know why the music faculty insisted on making this event a progressive concert. Having to manage the program and usher guests to four different stations around campus is a logistical challenge they are not up for."

"Well, you know, whatever Rider U does, we have to do. Can't let them get the best of us." Joel rolled his eyes in a good-natured way.

Grace chimed in from her office around the corner. "You know Blake's going to call you the night of and tell you he can't find his shoes. You should find out his shoe size and stock up now."

"She's right. This is going too far. You can't let these people get so dependent on you, or next year will be worse. When you go to the logistics meeting tonight, you have to let them figure out *all* of their problems. I'm begging you." Joel gave me a dramatic pleading pose, hands clasped in front of him in supplication. "Do not take on a single extra task. You have enough to do on Friday without, I don't know, hauling water bottles around."

I was exhausted, I was not sleeping, and I could barely think about next week, never mind next year. I held up a finger for quiet and made my call, getting the dean's voicemail. "Hello Dr. Plett, this is Evelyn Stone calling at four-thirty on Wednesday, confirming that you are prepared to give a welcome from the chapel stage at seven-thirty on Friday. Please keep in mind it should be no longer than three minutes, as the schedule is tight. Thank you!" I left my cell phone number and moved on to the next upper faculty member.

I had too much to do to argue with him, but I knew deep down that Joel was right. I needed to make a change. I marched into the logistics meeting armed with the courage of my convictions. I would not bend before the helplessness. I would not be swayed by tears. I would help them help themselves, like Jerry Maguire.

Aaron had been texting me regularly all week. While I waited for everyone else to show up, I pulled up my texts. Apparently, Joel had put out a bat signal because there was a new message from Aaron.

I hear you're about to be roped into a bunch of extra work.

I was going to murder Joel.

Joel shouldn't have texted you. It's none of his business

I almost added that it wasn't Aaron's either, but I didn't want to be too petty. The dots showed by his name.

I hope you won't take on too much, but I believe you can do it. Whatever you decide, you'll handle it.

Well, that was less annoying than Joel's constant nagging.

Thanks. I'm going to try to negotiate so I don't get stuck with too much extra. Wish me luck.

His reply came almost right away.

First rule of negotiation is to listen more than you talk. You're a great listener, so that's easy. The second is always get when you give. If you agree to do something for them, they have to take one of your tasks. Counteroffer, always. You got this. You don't need luck.

He sent me a winking emoji, blowing a kiss. I felt buoyed by that tiny heart and that little wink, and I rode that warmth all the way until I opened my meeting.

I led the agenda and got updates, and when Blake started complaining about who was going to post all the signage now that his coworker had the flu, I rallied all my remaining patience and prompted him to think of who else in his department could take over that responsibility. He eventually said I could ask the chamber choir to do it since they were performing in the second set. I let him know I'd be happy to do it if he wanted to take over calling the upper faculty. I didn't think it would work, but suddenly he was agreeing to call the choir members himself.

When the dust settled after the meeting, I only had three extra things on my to-do list, and I had given two of my tasks away. That was practically a miracle.

I texted Joel a simple "Snitches get stitches" with a knife and a skull. I was torn between being touched that I had so many people trying to look out for me and a stubborn insistence that I should be able to do this all on my own.

He sent back a sideways laughing/crying face. He found me not at all intimidating.

I was on to my next logistics meeting, and after to

the Archeology event I was hosting. Everything went smoothly and I was in a cab on my way home by ten p.m. I immediately changed and got ready for bed, and propped my swollen feet up on an extra pillow.

I checked my phone. Aaron had sent me a few encouraging words off and on all day.

I texted him good night while the phone screen blurred in front of my tired eyes. Only a few more days until the weekend.

SATURDAY MORNING WAS CRISP AND CLEAR, AND I saw none of it because I had gone to after midnight after Friday's event and slept in until noon. I woke to social media pictures of my friends out and about, the day sparkling around them, light bouncing in prisms off trees covered in hoarfrost.

Aaron had sent me a selfie bright and early of him at a job site; he had put up a mini tent around a patch he was doing on the outside of a building and had set up a heater so it would be warm enough for his cement to cure. His crew had the day off, but he was still on the job, finishing up.

He was pretty cute, with frost on his beard and his breath hanging in a cloud in front of his face. He squinted into the sun, bringing out the glints of green in his hazel eyes and the subtle tints of black in his brown beard.

I cropped it to just his face, saved the picture, and added it to his contact info. Then I sent it to Aunt Bea, just for good measure. She'd been asking about my "caller" in our text conversations. Her latest hashtag creation had been #dontdoanythingIwould-ntdo. I responded that it gave me enough wiggle room to drive a 747 through.

The sun was still out, and I hadn't missed the whole day. I opened all my curtains and let the light stream in.

It was time to deal with myself and my apartment. The kitchen was in a state I did not like to consider. I had to wash a spoon before I could have breakfast, eat my cereal out of a mug, and reuse the same mug for my coffee. Then I got down to tackling the dishes. There were more dirty dishes than I thought I had in my cupboards. I had to chip crusted food off the counter.

Aunt Bea called while I was in the middle of emptying my fridge to clean it. I put her on speaker so I could keep going, her high voice filling my kitchen. The sense of missing her was permanently lodged somewhere behind my breastbone, barely felt except when her voice brought it all to the fore.

"What a handsome young man you have!"

"Aunt Bea. He's not mine. We're just in each other's orbits for a while."

Her answering hum was skeptical. "Whatever you say. This is the first time you've talked about a special friend in the present tense. Even if you don't have him forever, you certainly seem interested in having him right now."

I didn't have an answer for that one. I was just grateful she hadn't called him my lover with rolled r's purred out at the end. With Aunt Bea, it was best to redirect. The conversation turned to what she and her dog Daisy had seen on their walk that morning, the interesting smells sniffed, the rude dog on the corner avoided.

"I think there may have been a crime committed near the Jensens' juniper bushes. Daisy was *very* interested in that spot, and I found the vibrations around the area disturbing."

"Maybe one of your neighbors is into public sex."

She liked that theory, though she claimed she wouldn't have been disturbed by the vibrations in that case because she was no prude. When I finally signed off and looked around my sparkling kitchen, I had a lightness in my step that only a chat with Aunt Bea could bring. Mum never felt so near as when I was cleaning, and nearer still with Aunt Bea in my ear while I was doing it. My sharpest pictures of her were with a rag in hand, yellow dish gloves on. We may not have had much, but our place was always spotless, just like my now clean kitchen. Satisfied, I took a nap on the couch with the TV on in the background.

When I woke up, Aaron's text was waiting for me.

Pick you up at 7:30 tonight?

I'll be ready

I had to get moving. It was already five, and I was groggy from my nap. I needed caffeine and a snack to tide me over and wake me up. During my long, hot shower, I shaved every part of me that I felt needed it, including a very thorough bush trim, just in case. I moisturized and blew my hair dry. My makeup was a cat eye and a deep red lip. I tidied my bedroom and bathroom, again, just in case.

I stood in front of my bedroom mirror and dressed carefully. My underwear was lace and didn't match my satiny plunge bra, but both were black. My faux-leather leggings were also black. The shirt I'd decided on was a deep, shimmery gold with a plunging V-neck, and the necklace resting right at the top of my cleavage drew the eye even more. I didn't want Aaron to look me in the eye all night.

Unfortunately, I was ready early—a rookie

mistake. It gave me too much time to pace. I paced in my living room, and then put my boots and coat on and stood in my entrance, shifting from foot to foot, peering out the window, looking for tall, wide-set headlights coming up my street.

Finally, he was there, right on time. Punctuality was a quality I greatly appreciated. I skipped down the cleared sidewalk and paused at the truck door. He'd put running boards on for me. The step up was a much more reasonable height. He'd been thinking of me. I sprung up and launched myself into his truck.

Aaron smiled at me, lit up by the warm glow of his cab lights for a moment before I shut the door and we were plunged into gloom. I beamed back and reached over to pull my seatbelt on. His hand was suddenly over mine on the seatbelt anchor. We clicked it in together, and then his gloved hand traveled up to my face, tipping my chin toward him like he couldn't wait to kiss me. I leaned in closer, tempting him, my giddy smile impossible to tamp down.

Our lips brushed. His eyelids were halfway down, savoring me. He dipped a little closer and pressed a little deeper, but when I started to move even closer to him, gripping the open edge of his jacket in my fist, he broke the kiss, seemingly remembering we were stopped in the middle of the street.

"Later," he said raggedly, and then paused, his hand still on my face. "I mean, I don't take anything for granted. If you don't want to invite me in later, I will be one hundred percent okay with that."

"Good to know," I said, a little coolly. I pulled back into my seat so he could start driving. I had never before had this feeling of being jerked around, getting heated up just to be left frustrated.

As soon as I had the thought, I realized how ungenerous it was. But he had brought me back to reality with a bump. He expected me to have words for him. He'd want a clear invitation. He wouldn't just sweep me away and rescue me from my overthinking brain.

But that was a problem for future me. In the meantime, I would try not to be a total bitch.

"I'm so glad it's the weekend." I carried on like nothing had happened. "I slept in till noon today, I was so tired from the week. It's good to go out with friends and just not think about work for a while."

"You don't have to answer your phone tonight?"

"No, I could keep checking it, but really if something was going to go wrong at the gala, it would have happened by now, and the staff there are really capable. There isn't going to be anything I can do that they won't be able to do."

He nodded, face flickering with light from every streetlamp we passed, a soft strobe over his strong features. "I'm glad you're letting it go."

"Don't think I haven't forgotten about you and Joel talking behind my back. You're both in trouble. Well, mostly him. You had some good advice."

"Yeah? We care about you." He slanted me a look under his brow at the next light. "And we're going to keep caring about you."

I huffed, putting on a show of annoyance, even while I melted inside, but he kept on. "Next time, talk to one of us before you go down a stress spiral. If you're talking to us, we won't be texting behind your back."

"I'll take it under advisement."

"Do that." His nod was confident that I would do so.

When we pulled up at the Lionshead, there wasn't a spot big enough for the truck.

"Run in, and I'll find parking. I won't be long."

Lazy snowflakes danced in the spotlight cast by each streetlamp. The beacon-yellow glow of the pub quickened my steps, light spilling generously from the windows and casting deeper shadows all around. I took a last bracing breath of cold air, drawing it deep. I couldn't keep the smile off my face. We were going to have fun tonight.

Chapter Twelve

❧

One of Grace's perfectly shaped eyebrows arched when she saw me, but she limited herself to a smirk and raised her glass in a mini toast.

"Nice rack, Stone," she drawled as I got to the table. "Any particular reason the girls are out tonight?"

"Holy shit, Evie," was what I got from Lucy, whose hair had gone from platinum to a silvery purple since the last time I'd seen her. "You look killer!"

Joel and Douglas came over from the table where they were racking up to say hi.

"Darling, for me? You shouldn't have," Joel said drolly, giving me a peck on the cheek. Douglas did the same, laughing both at Joel and at my blush.

"I doubt that neckline is for you, my love." He winked at me. "I wonder who it could be for?"

"Shut up, everyone. Yes, I look amazing. No, this cleavage is not for you, but feel free to enjoy it from afar. Preferably, very far."

I ordered a glass of wine when the server came over and started to catch up with Lucy while the others started a game. I had missed them the last few weeks. Lucy had just finished out a contract and was celebrating her payday. I clinked glasses with her as soon as my wine came.

I saw Aaron's big frame up at the front and started getting butterflies. I took another sip of wine, swallowing down my nerves.

He went to give back-slapping hugs to both of the men and a less aggressive hug to Grace and then came over to the table Lucy and I were sitting at. I saw the moment that he took in my top. He had raised a hand to say hi to Lucy and just stopped with it half in the air.

It was perfect. He was so dumbfounded I wanted to dance a jig on the spot. It would have the added advantage of making my breasts bounce. Maybe I should have, just to see his eyes pop.

He seemed to realize he was gaping with his mouth hanging open and shut it so hard I could almost hear the click. I hoped he hadn't bitten his tongue. I had a date with that tongue later.

He kept walking over, two spots of color high on his cheekbones, looking tense.

"Hi, Lucy," he said, leaning over to kiss her cheek. She gave him a side hug back, and I could see her eyes shining with suppressed glee.

"How are you, hon?" she asked.

"Just fine, you?" He sounded so casual, but he hadn't looked over at me again.

"Great!" She was all innocent enthusiasm. "Evie and I are just celebrating my payday. Come have a glass with us!"

She motioned between the two of us. His eyes followed the gesture, glued briefly to the expanse of skin I was showing, and then unstuck and hovered somewhere two feet behind me.

"Yeah," His voice was hoarse. "I'll just get a beer and join you."

He had no time to take refuge at the bar because the server was already coming over with a Guinness for him. Ha! That was the problem with having a regular place. There was no escaping these tits.

He sat down between us at the small round table, knees bumping my thighs. He unclenched his jaw enough to take a sip of his beer, after clinking glasses with both me and Lucy.

He picked up a menu, escaping with eyes down.

"So, what are you hungry for tonight?" My voice was a little too husky for it to be an innocent question.

Lucy coughed and made a fast escape. "Uh, I'm going to check out the game, guys. Order me a pound of hot honey wings."

Aaron looked up from his menu at me and got stuck on my breasts again and the pendant nestled right into the top of my cleavage. Finally, he made it all the way up to my eyes.

"What was the question?" He was in a daze, eyes glazed and dark.

I couldn't keep a straight face anymore. I started laughing. He glowered, brows down, but said nothing.

"I wanted to know what you're ordering. Since you're studying the menu so intently."

"Oh," he said. "Uh...I haven't taken it in. I've been a little...distracted. But I think you know that." He raised an eyebrow at me, and his eyes dipped down again like he couldn't help himself before coming back to my face.

I smirked in response. He glanced down at his menu again. "Wings sound just about right tonight."

I hummed my agreement and turned to my menu. When the server came over, we ordered enough for a crowd before sliding off our high bar chairs to join the others.

Aaron came up behind me and put his hands on my hips. He spoke into my ear, beard tickling at my neck.

"Is this okay? Or would you rather I not manhandle you in front of our friends?"

Our friends. Something about that gave me pause. It suggested a permanence that I had never before experienced. I shrugged mentally. I had already decided to go ahead despite the potential for it to get weird. My future was not set. I might not even be around the next season. So why not do something a little reckless, a little selfish, take pleasure for myself where I could find it, enjoy things while they lasted?

I looked around at the group again. Everyone was studiously giving us space, making me feel like we were in our own little bubble. The lights were low. Truthfully, I liked his hands on me. Truthfully, I wanted him to wind us both up until we didn't need any words between us.

I leaned back into him, my butt brushing up against him, my shoulders leaning back into his broad chest, his stomach soft against my lower back. I turned my head sideways, presenting more of my neck.

"I'm okay with it." I spoke softly, for him alone,

reveling in his answering groan and the way his fingers tightened on my hips.

"Wait, this was maybe a bad idea." He had a straight shot down my shirt over my shoulder, and I could feel his arousal through his jeans, pressed tight against me. The tension between us wound tighter, a spring under pressure, a rubber band stretched to breaking point.

Lucy eyed us sideways in between watching Douglas and Grace clear the pool table. Joel had darts in hand and was practicing his throws nearby, with mixed results.

She cleared her throat aggressively. "So, you guys gonna cool it? Or just bang one out right here on the pool table?"

I choked and pulled away from Aaron. He didn't let me get far but loosened his grip on my hips and draped one arm casually over my shoulder. I guessed that he was hiding some pretty damning evidence behind me and let him use me as a shield.

"Sorry, Lucy. We'll be a bit more chill." He didn't sound embarrassed at all.

"Thanks, man. I saw enough of you guys in college. I don't need to see any more pasty asses."

"Hey, the mooning phase was short-lived. We moved on eventually."

"Yes, thank god. But any amount of time was too

long. I'll never forget the time when Douglas stuck his ass out the car window right next to me. His grimy undies were fully down. I'll never unsee that. It haunts me to this day." Lucy ended her diatribe with a shudder while I cackled, bent over with laughter, and Aaron let out a loud "Ha!" that had the others coming over to see what we were going on about.

"You!" Lucy pointed dramatically at Douglas. "Traumatizing me forever with the sight of your bits!"

"Jeez, I'm glad you learned to keep it in your pants, Dougie." Grace drawled. "Lucy and I did not consent to seeing your pencil dick."

Douglas sputtered, hands in the air. "Pencil!" He couldn't seem to get anything coherent out. "And... and...that was years ago!"

"Aww, baby," Joel wheezed while putting an arm over Douglas' shoulders. "It's okay. I consent to seeing it whenever you want to show it to me."

Aaron and I were still laughing, his arm companionable around my shoulder, the tension between us dialed down to a more reasonable level. I was grateful to Lucy for taking the heat off me and distracting us.

Our food came before the trash talking had fully died down, and we all sat down and dug in.

"So, apart from mooning people, what other pranks did you get up to back in the day?" I was so curious about college life, tantalized by the glimpses I got to see on campus now, and by these friends still so close after all these years.

Douglas immediately launched into another tale of him and Aaron and Chris sneaking booze in a Gatorade bottle into their final lectures to celebrate the last day of class.

"All you have to do is drink a little out of the bottle, top it off with vodka, give it a shake. It's a 'life hack' because you hydrate and dehydrate at the same rate." Douglas looked pleased with his own brilliance, giving me a half bow in his chair when I slow-clapped for him ironically.

Joel hooted. "I think you killed off too many brain cells to evaluate whether you were hydrated or not."

"I wonder whether anyone's done a scientific study on drinking Gatorade and vodka together," Lucy mused thoughtfully, daintily but efficiently stripping down another chicken wing.

"If they have, I bet it was full of stats students. I think drinking was the only way we got through that class. I almost dropped it three times. Thank god Grace was there to help me cram at the last minute and pass that exam," Aaron said, shaking his head.

"Grace helped you, not Douglas? Why did he hang you out to dry?" I was desperate for these little glimpses of their college life.

"Well, the problem with Douglas is he's too good

with numbers. When something immediately makes sense to you, you can't teach it to anyone, because you haven't had to try to understand it. Right, D?"

Douglas shrugged, "Sorry. I tried to help. But I'm a terrible tutor. I can only explain it the one way it makes sense to me."

Lucy cleared her throat. "I have an announcement." She wiped her sticky fingers with a flourish, drawing out the suspense. "I have decided to buy a house." She received our enthusiastic congratulations and excited questions all piling on top of each other with pride, eyes shining with excitement. She, Aaron, Douglas, and Grace immediately launched into a discussion of mortgage rates and the percentage she should put down, whether she should do fixed-rate or variable. I understood a quarter of it. I looked across at Joel as the conversation flew across the table.

"Does this make any sense to you?"

"God, no. When we bought our house, Douglas handled those details. I just contribute my half and leave the rest up to him." They owned a house together and rented out the ground suite.

Aaron pulled out his phone to bring up his contacts and scribbled a name and number on the back of one of his business cards and handed it over to Lucy. "Call my cousin at the Lansdowne Credit Union. She'll get you a good rate. Tell her I sent you."

He paused, rubbing his beard in thought. "I'll ask my mom to call my aunt and let her know to expect you."

Was this seriously how things got done in small cities? At least I could be secure in the knowledge that Aaron seemed to have a relative or acquaintance in every sector if I ever needed anything. Homeownership as a somewhat achievable life goal for young professionals was another thing that still caught me off guard about living here.

Douglas had his phone out too, already on the real estate listings. "What area are you looking in? There's a house for sale right now on our street—I think it's a two-bedroom. I'll find the listing, but it looks well maintained from the outside."

"I'm looking for something closer to my parents. West end. If I can find something that doesn't have a huge yard in that area. I don't want to spend all my time cutting grass. It's the most useless plant."

I laughed at her disgusted expression. "It would be nice to have a garden plot for the summer. You could grow tomatoes! Herbs!" I tried to tone down the wistfulness in my voice.

"Oh, I don't have a green thumb at all," Lucy trilled. "But if I get a garden, you can come plant in it to your heart's content."

I smiled back. "I can't imagine busing to the west end of the city multiple times a week just to take care of a few tomatoes and some basil. That would be quite the garden commitment."

Grace chimed in. "Oh, Evie, I've been meaning to say, if you don't want to buy a car, there's a car co-op now. There's one parked near your place. The membership fee is really reasonable, and you only pay for the mileage you use." She grinned. "Maybe then you'd be able to garden wherever you wanted."

My smile froze on my face. People who lived here seemed to assume that everyone drove. "Grace, I don't have a license. I've never driven." At her confused look, I had to continue, even though I hated having to explain it. "There was a driver's education program in high school, but it cost extra, and it's not like we'd had a car to practice on."

I'd managed to blow up our happy chatter with that revelation. Everyone looked surprised, and was that a hint of pity in Joel's eye? The spotlight was fully turned on me again, picking out all my flaws in stark relief. My heart rate rose, the acrid tang of anxiety coating the back of my throat.

I thought I'd gotten past that feeling with this particular group of people. I opened my mouth to explain again, and stopped. Suddenly instead of being embarrassed at how I was once again lacking something that all of my friends had, I was annoyed.

Annoyed at the assumptions, annoyed at being a curiosity object.

I squinted around at them all accusingly. "You've all traveled outside the bounds of Elmdale. Do you need to drive when you visit Toronto? Not to mention Europe?" I waved in Aaron's direction. "Public transit is more reliable when you live in a city with actual population density. I don't know why you're all so surprised. There's lots of people even in this city that don't drive, so assuming that everyone should is extremely classist."

Eyes shifted around the table. I couldn't remember when I'd called anyone out seriously, other than when Joel had added me to the group chat without my permission. But that had been different than staring down this whole group of people. I was tired of swallowing down my objections, opinions, feelings. A tether somewhere in my soul had frayed and snapped.

Aaron shifted beside me so that he could look at me more head-on. "You're right, Evie. We shouldn't take it for granted. And you're right that we live in a city that doesn't prioritize transit, and it's a huge problem. I should know better than to be surprised."

Murmurs of assent came from the rest. I had shifted the mood, but when I looked over at each of them, all I saw was understanding. I was sure it had helped that Aaron had agreed with me; his word carried weight here. But it was more than that. I could actually feel their acceptance like a tangible thing, a comforting blanket. They respected that I'd stood up for myself, that I'd spoken my mind. I didn't need to swallow down all of my thoughts and feelings to be found worthy.

Grace reached out and squeezed my hand briefly in apology. "Sorry for making assumptions, Evie. And if you ever do want to learn to drive, you'll have a table full of volunteers to help."

"I'll be sure to let you know." I squeezed back before letting go. I knew it would be a good life skill to have, and the offer was appreciated.

"Let's return to the house hunt. I'd like to hear how many bedrooms Lucy is looking for." Douglas was gentle as he steered the conversation on to something less fraught.

Aaron's hand lay on the table next to me. It would have been casual if it hadn't been palm up, in silent invitation. I wasn't sure if he needed my touch to let him know I wasn't upset with him, or if he was tacitly offering me comfort or support. Either way, it was an invitation I didn't intend to pass up.

I slipped my hand into his, stroking his palm and intertwining our fingers, giving comfort and taking it in turn. His head had turned to answer Lucy's question, but I could see his cheeks rise with his smile, the hint of that half dimple coming out. It felt very domestic to sit there, holding his hand, casually affectionate, sipping the last of my drink and telling Grace more about my teenage years.

In between participating in the conversation, Aaron would look down at my hand in his and shoot a quick glance over at me, making sure I was still good. Over the course of eating, he seemed to have mastered the art of checking me out without gaping directly at my breasts. He was a fast learner, I'd grant him that.

We had only been there two hours, and everyone was done eating and talking and ready to play pool again. We left the tables, but Aaron drew me aside, tangling our fingers together again.

He looked down into my face, so serious. "Do you want to stay? Or do you want to call it and head back to your place?" He let go of my fingers and smoothed his hand up my arm like he couldn't help touching me, trailing up to my shoulder. His eyes flashed, and he openly took in my cleavage again. "I don't know if I'll be able to take it if you bend over a pool table tonight. It might kill me."

The fire in his eyes lit an answering fire in me. I was restless and ready to see what it would be like between us.

"Take me home, Aaron," I said, low but clear. His hand clenched around my upper arm and then gentled.

He turned to the others. "We're gonna head out, guys. I'll have to kick your asses at pool another night."

He got some good-natured groans, some exaggerated eye rolls, and a wolf whistle from Lucy. I should have been embarrassed that they all knew what was going down tonight, but I couldn't make myself care. I was practically floating on the sparks in Aaron's eyes, on the grip of his hand on my arm, on the way he lightly brushed his hands over my body as he helped me into my coat.

Chapter Thirteen

❦

I couldn't have said if we talked on the way to my place. I leaned sideways with my cheek on the warmed leather seats, taking him in. Drinking in the confident and attentive way he drove, illuminated in the intermittent flashes of the streetlights, big hands on the steering wheel, and his shoulders bunching and relaxing under his light jacket as he made the turns that would take us back to my place.

I was in a cocoon, protected from the world. In his truck, it was just us, drifting through the snowy darkness, the world muffled and hazy outside the frosty side windows, headlights fractured into sparklers through the windshield.

When we got to my street, it was of course packed full of cars. Aaron stopped in front of my place with his hazards on, then nudged my shoulder gently after seeing that I was still in a daze.

"If I go find parking, will you let me in the door?" He spoke lightly, but I thought for an instant I could hear the vulnerability behind the humor. Did he feel as cracked open as I did? I had to reassure him with as much as I could give.

"I'll be waiting for you. Don't worry." The chill knocked some sense back into me, and I went in to kill the minutes until he came bounding up the steps. It took such a short time that either there must have been parking on the next block or he'd run back. Or both.

I smiled and let him in, and he stamped the snow off his boots, hung a small bag beside his coat, and took me in again.

"Have I mentioned that I like your shirt?" Cheeky.

I grinned up into his face, not able to hold back my giddiness at having him in my place. "Hmm...not in so many words. But I got the gist."

He kicked off his boots and loomed close to me. "Ev. Let's make out." He stopped, seemingly unsure. "Sorry...I mean..."

I twined my arms around his neck to cut him short and pulled his face close. The sparks. I thought they would consume me whole. His eyes set me whirling. Suddenly words didn't seem so impossible as they had earlier.

"Let's. In fact, if you wouldn't mind, I'd be into some more bossiness tonight." I whispered the last into his mouth and leaned in for a long, hard kiss, swallowing his surprised huff before breaking away. "Why don't you come boss me around in the bedroom?"

He spun me around and practically dragged me down the hall, both of us laughing. My arms went back around his neck as soon as we arrived. It was delicious being pressed against his body, his face a breath away from mine, his long lashes half lowered as he took me in. He was staring down my shirt again, my breasts plumped up pornographically against his chest.

"See something you like?" I teased, still breathless.

His answer was a grunt. He unhooked my arms from around him and held them in one hand. His other arm became a supportive bar behind my shoulders as he leaned me back and took me in, releasing my hands so he could rest his on my chest, forearm nestled between my breasts.

"Bossy?" he whispered. "I think I can manage that." His big hand trailed ever so lightly up my chest to my neck, settling there for a moment. The subtle hint of dominance made me flush pink, and he saw it, noted the hitch in my breathing. He smiled in satisfaction, fingers tightening briefly before they trailed down and dipped into the front of my shirt.

It was his turn to flush. With color riding high on his cheeks, he followed the curve of my plunge bra down to my breastbone and back up the other side, thick fingertips grazing each barely covered nipple as he traced the edge of my bra. He groaned and gathered up one large breast in his palm, pushing it even plumper, then brought his whole face down to it. His beard abraded me softly, lightly prickling as he rubbed his cheek against my breast, breathing deep.

"Hell. You feel amazing. You smell amazing." His hand pushed me even rounder, and his teeth dug into the mound he had made. "You taste amazing."

He stepped back. "Take off your shirt, Ev." His voice sent shivers down my spine, raising goosebumps on my arms. There was a snap to his voice, but I knew it for a plea. His hands were fisted at his sides.

"Are you going to take yours off too?" I raised a brow in challenge.

"Sure." He shrugged, pulling his shirt off over his head in one motion. I laughed in pure delight. He'd misread my attempt at bratty playfulness. Maybe one day we'd get deeper into these roles, and he'd know each timbre and shift of my tone. For now, all I wanted to do was take him in.

He was glorious. Heavy with muscle, but not cut or sculpted, with a soft belly and hair on his chest that trailed down in a thick arrow. He stood still and let me take him in. I wanted to rub myself all over him like a cat on catnip. I lifted my top over my head. Fair was fair, after all.

I heard him inhale as I was still tangled in my shirt, my breasts jiggling with each movement. I could almost feel his gaze on them. When I got free, he was there, helping me throw my shirt somewhere into the corner of my bedroom. His arms wrapped around the small of my back and pressed me hard against him. I tugged away to get my hands free from between us and pulled his head closer, needing his mouth again. His kiss soothed and aroused, tempting me to sink even deeper into him. I caught my breath at his teeth grazing my lip, and his beard gently rasping my jaw while he found my bra clasp, releasing me. He ran his hands up and down my now bare back. I was obsessed with those glorious hands, so big and warm, melting and stimulating.

I couldn't get enough of touching him, his mix of hard and soft intoxicating. His shoulders were like boulders under my palms, but when I stroked down his fuzzy chest, he was more cushioned, with muscle firm underneath. I squirmed my hands down between us to the waistband of his jeans and tried to kiss him, rub myself against him, and get enough room to take off his pants, all at the same time. I was suddenly frantic and overloaded with sensation.

He took over, grabbing my hands in his, shushing me, and crowding me back toward the bed, until my knees hit the edge. He gave me a light nudge, and I tipped back, his hands still on mine slowing my fall. He had slid my bra off of my arms seconds later, and my hands were clasped firmly above my head in one of his as he gave me his weight to calm me.

"Now, are you going to let me explore this body?" he asked sternly, looking intently into my eyes. I nodded, trying to stay solemn, but couldn't keep my delight from lifting the corners of my lips. He was catching on. "Good. Keep your hands here."

My eyes fluttered partially closed until he was a blur in front of me. It helped to block him out at least a little—he was entirely too overwhelming. His chest hair tickled as he stretched over top of me then nudged my chin up and to the side so he could get to my neck. He spent several long moments licking, nibbling, and kissing up and down my neck and shoulders, scraping lightly with his teeth until I shuddered and gasped. I wrapped my hands around his head, holding him there, but he tsked and put them back up and out of his way.

Then his hands were cruising down my sides, starting at my elbows and stroking down to my waist before coming back up to brush the sides of my breasts. I arched up into his chest, hinting, looking for relief. He abandoned my neck and kissed his way down to my breasts, paying attention to the sensitive undersides before getting to my nipples, squeezing each one gently, giving them just the lightest edge of his teeth before increasing the pressure. He watched me closely the whole time, eyes hooded under his drawn eyebrows, taking me in completely, so careful, so sure, even now.

I panted and moaned, encouraging him to go harder, grinding against one of the big, muscular thighs he had thoughtfully shoved between mine.

He abandoned my nipples and kept traveling down my body, keeping one hand at my breasts, anchoring me as he kissed his way down my soft rolls. He got to my leggings and paused, pressing the heel of his hand firmly on my clit through the fabric with sweet pressure. Relief flooded me for an instant before my arousal kicked up again and I needed so much more.

"This okay?" he asked through gritted teeth, both

hands now hooked in the waistband of my leggings, eyes on mine, checking in.

"Yes. Hell yes. If you don't get inside me soon, I will die."

He huffed a chuckle. "We wouldn't want that."

He kissed his way down my hips as he stripped me efficiently. He stood up for a moment to take me in. I squirmed, stretched out naked in front of him, arms overhead, breasts softly falling to each side, legs squeezing together trying to get the pressure I needed.

"You are fucking gorgeous, Ev." His voice was a reverent whisper, his eyes still sparking, but I was not having any of it.

"Get to work, Aaron. I need you now."

He laughed again and obediently knelt at the edge of the bed, pulling me closer and settling between my legs, draping my knees over his shoulders and getting comfortable. He started to tease me, blowing softly on my clit, nibbling around it, turning his head and sinking his teeth into my thigh, going everywhere except where I needed him. His hands were underneath me, kneading, his thumbs so close to where I wanted them I could scream.

I grabbed his head in both hands. He looked up at me through his brows, his look of concentration stealing my breath, nose brushing my clit lightly, pressing his bearded chin into me, scraping against me deliciously. I trembled. He was winding me up, but I had nowhere left to go. He let me guide his face down again and started a slow twirl of his tongue around my clit before sucking in a steady rhythm. It was sweet relief. He adjusted subtly until he found the spot and the rhythm that sent my hips off the bed.

He encouraged me with his hands on my ass, supporting me as I flew higher. I broke apart screaming, my orgasm tearing through me as I curved around his face, thighs squeezing together. He let me ride it out and come down slowly.

I flopped back onto the bed gracelessly, limbs heavy. Aaron paused to wipe his beard on his discarded shirt before coming up to join me. I appreciated the thoughtfulness. He settled beside me on his side, hands stroking over me, up and down smoothly, taking in the feel of me, giving me time to recover.

"How was that?"

He still had his jeans on. I rolled onto my side and kissed him, pulling him down half onto me, my free hand roaming over all of him that I could reach. I traveled down to his jeans, feeling him hard behind his fly, and was again impatient to see him.

"I think it'll do, for a first round."

I struggled to open the button one-handed and growled in frustration into his mouth, still kissing him. He took over, not breaking our kiss, undoing his fly and shoving his jeans partially down, just enough for me to get my hands on him at last. He groaned into our kiss and bucked into my touch, his hand flexing around my arm. He was smooth and thick and utter perfection, as I gripped him with my hand in his underwear, skin sliding up and down.

I pushed his shoulders back, needing to see all of him. He obliged me and leaned back with both hands behind his head, making his biceps bulge out, propping his head enough to watch me. He was laid out before me like a banquet table, cock partially out, laying dark against his belly. I couldn't imagine a more perfect sight.

He helped me strip off his clothes, kicking his jeans off while I sat at his hip and caressed him. He let me play, exploring the soft velvety head, cupping his testicles gently, before going back to his shaft and grasping more firmly.

It was his turn to pant now, thrusting up into my hand, and his turn to put his hand on the back of my head and coax me closer. I shifted to get better access and hovered above him, teasing him, my lips an inch away from where he wanted them. He thrust up to touch them and groaned again when he made contact.

"Ev," he said roughly. "Suck it, or get on top of me."

Bossy. I licked my lips provocatively and gave him my brattiest smile, leaning further into the role, inviting him to play along. He whimpered and put a little more pressure on my head, and I let him guide me down on to him, swirling my tongue around the head before sucking him into my mouth. His hands fell away to the bed, fists deep in the mattress as he arched up, his body a straining line. He was magnificent. I could have watched him for hours. I was going to turn this man inside out before I was through with him.

I released him with a noisy pop and then repeated the motion, just for fun. I paused to lick my lips again and heard him whimper.

"I have condoms in the side table," I said archly, then bent back down, sucking and swirling, just like he had done to me. He reached over and got a condom, then pushed me back so he could put it on, his shaking hands filling me with immense satisfaction.

"How do you want it?" He lay with heavy-lidded eyes, erection still in hand, pointing it straight up.

"I want you on top." I could think of nothing better than his weight on me.

He had me on my back right away and pushed straight into me, one hand under one of my knees, holding me open, the other holding most of his weight off me.

He looked down our bodies, taking me in, lifting up to watch himself slide into me, before looking back at my face. Our eyes connected. His were all sparks. I ached at the tender intensity I saw there, the reverence, the awe. One slow slide, two, and then we found our rhythm together. I dug one heel into his thigh and planted the other foot on the bed for leverage. We moved together, him stroking into me with deep, sure rhythm, me rising to meet him and grind my clit against him at the top.

He lit me up inside at all the right spots until I was shaking and trembling and on the verge of another orgasm. I pinched my nipples, hard. Harder than I would normally have done, but I was so close to orgasm that all pain was pleasure. I cried out as I came again, and he rode it out, slowing after I went limp.

"Turn over," he said, after I had come down a little further.

I was loose-limbed and slow, so he arranged me as he wanted me, facing the mirror on the other side of the room, nudging me up to kneeling until I was fully exposed to him. He lined us up and thrust straight in again, only pausing to make sure I was okay before he started in earnest, pulling my hips back to meet him with each thrust, his pelvis slapping against me. I lifted my head to watch him in that perfectly placed mirror. He was staring down at himself thrusting into me, fully absorbed, and I was jealous that he got to watch. His chest and arms were magnificently corded with the effort of holding himself together, and his eyes were black pools. After two more hard jerks, he came, gasping my name like a prayer, squeezing my hips in a vice grip.

We couldn't collapse together until after he had dealt with the condom and I'd gone to the bathroom. The bed was one hundred percent more comfortable with him taking up more than half of it. I should have felt claustrophobic, but instead I was comforted. He belonged under my covers.

I put my head on his shoulder and slung a bare leg over his. "I need to put mirrors on every surface of this room," I said sleepily. "Maybe you should buy a GoPro." I yawned through the last word.

"Oh?" He sounded amused, nuzzling his face into my hair. "And why is that?"

"You get to see everything. I want your view when you're behind me. I want to see what you see."

"Hmm. So should we hook up a live feed for you? I can tell you, the view was amazing."

"Yes, I'd like that. Set that up for next time." I was already half asleep but I felt his laugh rumble through his chest as he snuggled me closer.

Chapter Fourteen

❦

I woke to bright light in my face. We'd forgotten to close the blinds last night. I realized I hadn't even brushed my teeth or washed my face. That never happened. I turned my head. Aaron was awake, staring at me from inches away, very much alert. He had stayed. Of course he had.

I blinked. "You've been awake a while, haven't you?"

His teeth flashed in his smile, the full sun picking out the black in his brown beard. "My internal clock is too strong. But I didn't want to wake you. Good morning, sleepy." He leaned in for a soft but thorough kiss.

"Good morning." I didn't bother suppressing my answering smile. His was too infectious to be ignored.

He got up and walked naked to the bathroom, completely unselfconscious.

The bright light of morning streamed into the room, lighting up all the places where last night we had been so brazen, garishly highlighting our discarded clothes, the partially open drawer revealing a ripped open box of condoms. Everything was raw and exposed.

This was not how it should be. Mornings were for awkward goodbyes in dim early light, for rushed leave-taking and meaningless promises.

I leaped up and scuttled to my dresser like a crab looking for a new shell home. Finding one of my bras, a tank, and some leggings, I hurried into them, not knowing how long he would take in the bathroom.

He came out, still naked, moments after I was dressed. He took me in with a raised eyebrow, and stood there, semi-hard. I knew I was gaping at him, two bright burning circles on my cheeks. I didn't know how to do this. Panic rose.

Brushing past him, I shut myself in the bathroom, going straight to the sink to run cool water, splashing it on my face and the back of my neck. My chest was tight and constricted. My heart was pounding in my ears.

Breathing. I needed to do it. I felt Aunt Bea's hand on my shoulder, taking me back to hospital waiting rooms, her voice in my ear talking me through my thick panic. Four things I feel. The vinyl floor under my feet. The water dripping down my face. The band of my bra. The cool edge of the sink under my hands. My chest finally loosened a fraction, enough for me to breathe in for a count of four and out for a count of eight. I did it again.

Okay. Okay. I was okay.

A knock at the door. "Everything alright? I have clothes on now, so you don't need to worry about me jumping you."

He was too perceptive. "It's fine, I'll be out in a bit. Why don't you make us some coffee? Go ahead and rummage through the cupboards."

A pause stretched. "Okay. I'll be out there rummaging. Yell if you need me." His voice was muffled by the door, and I couldn't tell what he was thinking, whether he was upset. Prickles of panic still lingered around the edges of my brain, a tingle in my limbs and tightness in my chest.

I felt fresher after brushing my teeth and scrubbing the makeup off my face. My liquid lipstick had settled into the cracks of my lips, and my eyeliner had shifted into alarming new territories. I had to change into another tank top because of all my water splashing. I put my cozy wool cardigan over it and pulled on wool socks. Properly armored, I went to find coffee and hopefully some fortitude.

Aaron had made himself at home in the kitchen. Barefoot, wearing only a T-shirt and jeans, the temperatures in my creaky old apartment didn't seem to bother him. It was always chilly in the morning, the wind getting into cracks under the door or seeping in through the single-pane windows overnight. But he looked as comfortable as ever.

The coffee pot was burbling, nearly done already, and he had toast in the toaster, which he pushed down when he saw me coming. There was butter foaming in a hot pan as he cracked an egg into it. I saw another plate of eggs already made beside the stove.

"I hope you don't mind me using the eggs. It seemed like the fastest option."

"No, that's fine. Sunday is grocery day anyway. And the corner store is open if we need anything." The coffee pot beeped, and I got us both mugs. "What do you take?"

"Do you have cream?"

"No, sorry. I usually drink mine black. I have some milk, I think."

He nodded and finished up the eggs. I poured both of us mugs and added a good splash of milk to his, not sure what his ideal coffee color was, and took them to my tiny dining table. I usually ate on the couch, but after-sex breakfast called for more formal dining. He brought over two plates with buttered toast and eggs and set them down with a brief kiss to my temple. My eggs were steaming, and his were not.

"Sorry you're eating cold eggs. You didn't have to wait for me."

"I wanted to wait. And I don't mind lukewarm food. It still tastes fine. I wasn't sure how many you wanted"—he gestured at my plate—"but most people order two eggs, so I started there."

He was a hungry bear-man, digging into his breakfast. I had the sudden thought I would enjoy cooking for him. If I were cooking for him, I wouldn't have to eat leftovers for days on end. I quashed that domestic thought. I was not about to coo over him like a grandmother and urge him to eat, but now I understood the impulse. Food was pleasure and comfort, and sharing it with someone else was like sharing love. It was harder to quash that thought.

I caught Aaron eyeing me like I was a ticking time bomb, and I realized I was just staring at my eggs, eyes swimming, overwhelmed by feelings. All my circuits were overloaded, the screen flashing "ERROR."

"Hey." He gently interrupted my circuit meltdown. "It's okay. Eat your breakfast. Drink your coffee."

He took a bite of his toast, and the appealing crunch prompted me to turn back to my plate. My eggs had cooled while I was having my tiny existential crisis. They were sunny-side instead of the much superior over easy, demonstrating that he had major flaws that I would continue uncover if he stuck around. I dipped my toast into the yolk.

"What's your plan for today, other than groceries?" Aaron asked between bites, looking satisfied to see me eating.

"I have some work to check on, and I usually clean a bit, get ready for the week, plan meals, and cook."

"Sounds like a nice quiet day."

"I like to feel prepared for the week. What about you? Are you going to your parents' place?"

"I was thinking of sticking around today. I hear the highways are icy." He paused and glanced at me casually from under his brows. "We could both get some work done today. Pick up groceries, stop at my place to get my computer and a few files. Make supper together later."

He was so carefully casual, I wondered if he felt like he was swimming in shark-infested waters, not knowing what would set me off into a meltdown.

"Oh? And what about after supper?" I was arch as I picked up my last bite of toast and went over to sit on the couch with my coffee mug. I could be casual too. My coffee was the perfect temperature—still hot, but not scalding.

"I was hoping you'd ask me to stay. I'd probably pack another bag in my truck, just in case. But I'd need to get up around five." He was sheepish, not looking at me as he set his fork down and picked up his mug to join me.

It was the most natural thing in the world to turn and put my feet in his lap. More natural yet for him to wrap one warm hand around my foot and press his thumb into my arch, sipping his coffee all the while. His touch grounded me, making my earlier panic seem trivial and distant, like it had happened to someone else.

It gave me the confidence to tell him he could stay. "I don't mind you getting up early. I'll probably be able to go back to sleep. And if not, at least I'll be awake for work."

We stayed on the couch, sipping coffee, while I made my grocery list. Aaron had his ready on his phone, but I was old-school. I added a carton of cream and, after thinking for a minute, meat to make a shepherd's pie. Maybe I could fuss over him a just little, since he'd made me breakfast.

Aaron's version of getting ready for the cold was to put on a pair of socks and grab a thin hoodie from his bag. I thought I ran warm, but he was something else entirely.

Our errands took a surprisingly short amount of time. We were in and out of the grocery store in record time, Aaron pushing the cart for both of us, keeping our sections separate. We stopped by a cafe for fancy coffees and pastries. Then we went to Aaron's house. Reports of it being close to my place, or of my place being on the way to the pub, had been greatly exaggerated.

It was a sturdy little house in a neat area full of seventies-style bungalows. Very different from my area where all the houses were all well over a hundred years old, with the creaks to prove it. He had two bedrooms, one of which he'd turned into an office. I looked around as he packed a bag. The kitchen looked out of date, but the walls had been painted a cheery shade of red and the wood cabinets done in white. The living/dining area was gray with a darker blue-gray accent wall, with the same color echoed in his furniture. I wondered if he had painted it, or if it had been move-in ready.

I could hear Aaron moving through the back of the house, packing, gathering his files. It felt so weird standing there in his kitchen listening to him that I had to move to distract myself.

I wandered down the hallway and peeked into the bathroom. It was done in tile—floors in a dark slate gray stone, walls in a lighter shade, and shower tiled in a pretty blue scallop that looked like fish scales. It was the most updated of any room I had seen so far.

I opened his vanity to snoop. It was all standard: a bottle of vitamin D—sensible of him, in this climate —a razor and a small electric trimmer, face lotion, beard oil, shaving cream, a spare bar of lemon verbena soap, and deodorant. He had a tin of a yellow salve that claimed to seal deep skin cracks. I imagined that working with stone dried out your skin.

Aaron was suddenly at the bathroom door, catching me rifling through his beauty products.

"Enjoying your self-guided tour?" he asked wryly.

"Yes, thank you." My tone was regal and gracious. "However," I continued, after a dramatic pause, "you could provide one of those museum-tour recordings to highlight points of interest. For next time."

He laughed and shook his head. "I'll keep it in mind for future improvements. So, what do you think of the place?"

"Very nice. Just the right amount of space."

He nodded appreciatively. "That was why I decided to buy it. It's got some yard but not too much, and it was new enough that I didn't need to do much to it."

"Did you renovate the bathroom?"

"Yeah, I had to do that one. They hadn't changed it since the original build, so it was time. You should have seen the paneling and the pink toilet and the tiny tub. I had to keep my elbows tucked in the shower."

"It looks great, Aaron. I love the colors."

He beamed at me. "I have a buddy who's a tiler so we traded some work. His wife is a designer, and she helped me put together what I wanted. I'm happy with how it turned out."

"Must be nice to have connections." We smiled at each other, and then both seemed to realize we were still standing in his bathroom at the same time.

"I'm ready to head out. Do you want to get going? Or do you need a longer tour?"

"Nah, I'll find the bodies in your basement another time."

He scoffed and elbowed me. "I keep them in the backyard, like a normal person."

"Creep." I shoved him lightly back with my elbow and waltzed ahead.

Chapter Fifteen

❧❧❧

Our afternoon together at my place was productive and companionable. I adjusted my spreadsheets and to-do lists and sent out emails to the different events teams so they would be ready with updated information come Monday morning. Aaron worked on his budgeting and did up a few quotes. Then he stretched out on the couch and closed his eyes while I finished up.

I would have finished faster if he hadn't distracted me, his body so comfortable stretched on my couch that I wanted to climb on top of him and take a nap too. He had crossed his arms on his chest to keep them from hanging off the edge, his biceps bulging appealingly against his T-shirt.

His face was in profile, strong brow and nose, full mouth, and luxurious brown beard. I took out my phone and snapped a quick picture. I couldn't resist the way he looked, relaxed like he was under a spell, a sleeping prince. Maybe he was. But if I had enchanted him, I would be the witch in this scenario. The metaphor broke down quickly. I shook my head at myself and went back to work.

His eyes opened when he heard me stacking my notes and packing away my computer. He sat up a bit and beckoned me over, and when I came close enough, he tugged me down onto his lap, chuckling at my shriek of surprise and cuddling me against his chest. We didn't speak. We hadn't spoken much the whole day. I didn't know who was giving space to whom, but I decided not to overanalyze it.

I sighed and sank further into him, his front cushioning me, my head on his shoulder, my feet propped up on the couch beside us. I lifted one hand and brought it to his face, feeling his beard under my palm and ruffling his short hair with my fingers. He leaned into my hand for a moment. When he spoke, his voice rumbled through me in a way that was becoming my favorite sensation.

"If we get the cooking done now, we can relax the rest of the evening." He was kneading my neck lightly with one hand, the other resting heavily on my knee. I never wanted to move again, but he made a good point.

I sighed and nodded against his chest. He smacked my thigh lightly twice, encouraging me to get a move on, and I did so, grumbling.

It was fun to cook with someone else for a change, learning how to dance around each other in the kitchen. Aaron chopped onions and peppers, and I started cooking chicken for my work lunches. Then we did a big sauté with the onions and peppers and Tex-Mex style seasoning, adding beans, rice, and salsa. Topped with cheese, avocado, lime, and hot sauce and scooped with tortilla chips, it was a satisfying supper. I smiled to see Aaron digging in and going back for seconds. I had decided that a lazy day together meant we could go back to informal dining, so we ate together on the couch with the TV on in the background.

Aaron made me tea when we were done. We sat together, snuggled up like we had been the first day he came over. His presence then had been so low-key, I'd been lulled into crawling into his lap and getting comfortable. Now I knew just how keyed up he could get, and how magnificent a sight it was to see.

I realized I was stroking his arms where he held me, admiring the topography of his veins and tendons as I brushed over the slight roughness of chapped skin at his knuckles. I needed these hands on me.

Turning into him, I rose enough to take his face

in both hands and kiss him. A dreamy trance took over, fuzzing the edges of my perception and sharpening every sensation between us. Clocks stopped. There was only this kiss, this touch, this moment. I reveled in the feel of his arms tightening around my waist, his hands spreading over me like he was trying to absorb me through his palms. Slowly, our dreamy kiss got more desperate, urgent—tongues tangling, teeth nipping. I sucked his bottom lip in between my teeth and let it go slowly.

He groaned, grabbed the back of my head, and swept his tongue into my mouth. His hands had made their way under my shirt now, up underneath my band when he discovered there was no clasp to undo. He squeezed my ribs briefly before coming around to cup under my breasts, weighing them in his palms, squeezing them together. He trailed his fingers over the tops of my breasts where the lacy edge met flesh, my nipples hard in his palms and begging for his attention.

I didn't want to lose myself into his hands yet. No, I wanted to take him completely apart, make him strain and whimper. Today, I was taking charge of this runaway train of lust. It was all within my power, and I was going to prove it, to him and to me.

I pulled away from his mouth to whisper in his ear. "I'm going to get a condom. When I get back here, I expect you to be naked." I may have had to gulp for air every few words, but I thought I sounded properly commanding.

I found the condom in my bedside drawer, and when I got back, he was naked on the couch, waiting for me. So obedient. I wanted to coo at his compliance. Instead, I tossed the condom onto his naked belly.

"Put it on," I ordered, before starting to strip. I unbuttoned my sweater slowly, letting it slip off my shoulders, and grabbed the hem of my tank. He had stopped with the condom package half ripped, erection bobbing against his stomach as he watched me. I paused in undressing and raised an eyebrow at him until he kept going with his task.

I pulled my tank off but left my soft lace bralette on, the deep V highlighting my cleavage. The big muscles of his thighs bunched as he rolled the condom down. His mouth was tight behind his beard, his brows drawn as he looked back at me, still holding his erection, watching me with wary intensity.

I wriggled out of my pants, taking my underwear with them, and let him look at my mostly naked body.

"Fuck, you're sexy." His voice was hoarse again. That edge was gratifying. I needed to know that I affected him as much as he affected me.

I smirked while I posed with a hand on a hip and let him look his fill, not bothering to hide my soft belly rolls. His eyes darted here and there, lingering on my cleavage, trying to catch a glimpse between my thighs, meandering down my legs to my toes before traveling back up.

My smile grew as I stepped closer, his hand catching me behind a thigh as soon as I was close enough, urging me on to his lap. Straddling him was starting to feel like familiar territory, but straddling him naked with his condom-covered cock trapped hard between us was a new dimension unlocked.

His hands were everywhere. Under my thighs, urging me higher. On my breasts, kneading, mounding, finding my nipples through the lace. Pulling me forward with a firm press on my back, bringing my breast to his mouth to nip and suck. The wet lace rubbed against my nipple when he switched to the other side.

He had taken control easily once I was within grabbing range, messing with my mild attempt at dominance, playing with my body like it was his to use. I had to wrest back control before I melted completely.

I leveraged myself up with my hands on his shoulders and settled on his erection, wiggling around until he was seated deep inside me. His mouth was at my neck now, teeth scraping and making me shiver, one hand clamped on my back, the other firm at my hip. He pinned me to him and curled deeper up into me, tense and pulsing, the strain on his face telling me he was fighting for control.

I was determined he would lose that fight completely. I pushed at his heavy shoulders and arms, and he loosened them immediately, looking at me with concern.

"Did I hurt you?"

"No." I was curt, focused on my goal. "Keep your hands off me now." They fell away immediately, his face worried. He was about to speak again, but I interrupted, my voice soothing. "Hush now. I have something to do."

I leveraged myself up again with my hands on his shoulders, pushing him further back into the couch and sliding up until only the tip of him was inside me. Then I started to ride him, first slow and leisurely, then faster, long strokes, then short ones, settling into a rhythm.

His hands were on me again like he couldn't help himself, cupping my ass lightly, letting me set the pace and feeling me slide down on him. His eyes were everywhere—burning into mine, watching my mouth, staring at my breasts swaying in front of him. He couldn't get enough of me. I felt like I could topple cities and conquer planets. The power flowing through me at having him laid out and helpless before me was heady, intoxicating.

He was starting to glaze over, closing his eyes, his head drifting back, hips pumping up to meet me, hands tightening on my hips and pulling me down harder onto him. He opened his eyes again, desperate, pained, on the edge.

"You need to stop unless you want me to come." His voice was a rasp and a desperate plea. His fingertips would leave marks. His collarbones were hollowed out with the tension, pecs carved sharper with each heave of his chest. He was gorgeous.

"I want you to come," I panted, getting closer to the edge myself, grinding down on him a little harder, raking my fingernails across his chest.

My connection to him in that moment was so strong as I looked into those heavy-lidded hazel eyes, I could almost see the razor edge he was on, almost feel the spring snapping as he came. He groaned and arched up into me again, hands moving me in short strokes as he finished, his head thrown back again, the veins of his neck corded up to where they disappeared into his beard.

We collapsed together, panting from our efforts, his hands resting heavily on my spine. I kissed his fuzzy chest affectionately. Seeing him come apart was extremely satisfying, but I was still tingling and throbbing. I pressed into him and squirmed, trying to subtly get some relief.

He gave me a smack on my bottom, loud but not painful. "Not with the condom still on. Go meet me in the bedroom."

I got another smack, and by his satisfied smile, he enjoyed the way the sound rang and the way my ass shook when he did it. He was irresistible. I pulled him down into another kiss, until he reminded me with another smack to get moving. He held the condom at the base while I extricated myself awkwardly from his lap.

I went straight to my bedside drawer and opened wide, all my toys on display in a not-so-subtle hint. I lay back with my smallest vibe on low so that I wouldn't come without Aaron.

I was lost in his eyes in my memory, sliding my vibrator in tight circles around my clit, feeling empty without him inside me. I looked over, alerted by a quiet creak of floorboards. Aaron stood in the door watching me, his erection hanging down now, softer. His shoulders and chest had a sheen of sweat that caught a gleam from the hall light. He was so magnetic, he made me ache.

I held out my hand, and he joined me, taking in the toys I'd left on display. He picked up my thickest and brandished the bright blue length with a wicked gleam in his eyes before settling down on the bed and pushing my legs wide with the breadth of his shoulders.

"How do you want it?"

I could barely breathe seeing him between my thighs, lit up with enthusiasm, focused on my pleasure.

"You decide." I was surrendering control back, confident he would make it worth my while.

He started to fuck me slowly with the dildo, eventually pushing my hand with the smaller vibrator aside and replacing it with his mouth on my clit, sucking, teasing, pinching softly between his teeth. All the while, his hand kept up the pace, pushing in and out, lighting me up from the inside. All I could do was hang on, gripping his head in one hand to keep him there, bracing myself against the headboard with the other, my whole body moving to the rhythm he had set. I came hard, gasping for breath, vision going white as the stars exploded behind my eyes.

Aaron soothed me and petted me, helping me ride out my aftershocks until I lay limp and spent, then gathering me up into his arms.

"How was that?" His whisper in my ear held a contented note.

I patted his shoulder with one still-floppy hand. "Pretty darn good. And for you?"

He chuckled. "You wrecked me. I'll never be the same. Feel free to do it again."

He leaned down to kiss the smug smile off my lips before pushing up to go wash off my toys and clean up. I could see him through the open door across the hall, searching for a washcloth and carefully wiping each toy down. I could practically picture the look on his face, the careful concentration. The man never seemed to do anything by halves.

After he was done, I got up and dragged myself through my bedtime routine, determined not to miss another night of skincare. Finding a clean sleep shirt in my drawer, I crawled into bed beside Aaron.

He immediately pulled me into his arms, arranging my limp body like his own personal body pillow, and dropped straight into sleep with the lamp still on. It was extremely comfortable, until the dead weight of his big arm started to press so heavily on my ribs that I couldn't take a full breath. I nudged him off me. He rearranged us without waking up, snuggling my butt closer to him. I yawned and closed my eyes. That sleepy nuzzle on my neck was getting addictive, as was his heat at my back. It wouldn't hurt to savor this just a little bit longer.

Chapter Sixteen

❧

He was gone when I woke the next morning. I found a note on my pillow. "Good morning, beautiful. I hope you have a good day. Aaron." It was simple and direct, like he was. It warmed me to picture him moving around in the dark winter morning, finding a pen and paper, and coming carefully back on my creaky hardwood floors to leave it beside my bed. Had he leaned down for a kiss, or had he not risked waking me?

I got ready for work with a hum in my throat and a spring in my step. I had been ignoring the messages from the group chat and the individual texts from Grace and Lucy. Those two had been nonstop in my phone all Sunday, sending eggplants, winking emojis, innuendo, demanding updates, threatening murder— usual friend stuff, I was sure.

I knew they didn't actually want the details of what we'd been doing, but I thought this joking around was their way of showing me they were excited, happy for me. I was excited for me too. I had decided during breakfast that I was going to ride this little fling out as long as I could. Even if it was a little more intense than what I was used to, it couldn't hurt to have fun for a while, to exchange pleasure, comfort. After all, he and Lucy had dated and been perfectly friendly after. Maybe it could even turn into a friends-with-benefits kind of thing as long as he was single—mind-blowing, clit-exploding casual sex would be a nice change from the rum-fueled gambles I used to take.

The walk to work that morning was delightful despite the way the cloudy gray sky and dull snow blended on the horizon, making it feel like the city was set in a particularly uninteresting black and white movie. The temperatures were mild, thanks to all the cloud cover, and the sidewalks were well trampled. The scenery went mostly unnoticed, preoccupied as I was with the beautifully pornographic reel playing in my head, reliving my weekend with Aaron, thinking of all the things we could try and do and play together. Taking him apart and watching him lose control had been delicious. I couldn't wait to do it again. Casually, of course.

When I got into the office, Joel and Grace were both waiting at the front desk for me, like the stalkers they truly were. Melanie was eyeing both of them doubtfully, and looked relieved that I had arrived to take the maniacs off her hands. I waved at her and hung up my coat, my watchers tracking my every move.

"So, Joel," said Grace, terribly casually, "did you get *up* to anything fun this weekend?"

"Hmm," Joel answered in his most serious tones, "I don't believe that anything *comes* to mind. If anything *popped u*p, of course I would tell you."

"These emphases are unnecessary," I said, with great dignity. I walked into my office and shut the door behind me, only barely getting behind my desk before they both barged in. They lost a moment because they were both trying to open the door and fit through at the same time. Now they shut it behind them and pulled up in the chairs in front of my desk, moving in sync like the twins from *The Shining*. I shook my head at them, genuinely creeped out by this intensity of purpose.

"Spill it, Stone." Grace's voice cracked like a drill sergeant.

Joel leaned forward sympathetically, good cop to her scary cop. "How did it go with Aaron after you guys left?" His eyes gleamed with fervor. I changed my mind and decided he was the scary one.

"You do both have work to do, right?" They stared back at me, waiting me out. "Fine. What do you want me to do, describe the length of his dick?" I really was getting comfortable with them.

"We—No!" They were both spluttering now. I sat back smugly. Now who was embarrassed?

"We may not want all the details, but we do want to know something," Grace said primly. She ruined it by cupping her hand beside her mouth and continuing in a dramatic stage whisper, "You can tell me about his dick later." She cackled when Joel slapped at her arm.

"That's my friend you're creeping on. He's like a brother to me. And I am not into brother stuff."

"Shoulda thought of that before you got all nosey." My tone was lofty. "Seriously though, it was an amazing weekend. We hung out all day yesterday. We even did chores and errands. He stayed over again last night. He must have been stealthy when he left this morning because I didn't wake up at all. He's very thoughtful like that."

There, that wasn't too mushy or overly descriptive. If I sounded a little dreamy by the end of it, it was understandable. I was still under the spell of the very good sex I'd had that weekend.

Grace and Joel exchanged looks I didn't know how to interpret. I wasn't going to give them the satisfaction of asking.

"I'm glad you're having a good time together," Grace said gently. "You're right, he is thoughtful."

I narrowed my eyes at her. Was it my imagination, or was there a hidden "but" in that sentence?

"Have you had the talk yet?" Joel asked, distracting me.

I looked at him blankly. "About what?"

"I'll take that as a no," Joel drawled. "DTR? Define the Relationship?" I could hear the capital letters he'd put on that phrase.

"Please. We're just having a casual thing. We won't need to talk about it."

Grace pursed her lips. "If Aaron doesn't have major plans already, I'd be very much surprised." She leaned forward at my probably horrified expression. "Evie, I'm not trying to freak you out. Just trying to prepare you. Aaron always has a plan. A five-year plan, and a ten-year plan."

Joel looked at Grace, puzzled. "Why would that freak her out?"

Maybe I should have left it to Grace to answer for me. What was up with me that I could condense into a soundbite for his benefit?

"I'm just not sure how long I'll be living here, or

of my future plans. I'm keeping it casual for now." There, that should be enough to satisfy him.

"Why wouldn't you be here? You have a different job in mind?"

Or not. We all sat in silence for a minute. Awkward. I didn't know how to tell them that I couldn't imagine my life in five years at all, that my future was a question mark, a black hole. It loomed ever nearer on the horizon, swallowing stars.

Grace rescued me from the frightening void of space. "It's okay, Evie. You don't need to define anything yet. It's okay to take things slow."

I nodded, but I wanted to protest. Taking things slow implied there was something we were taking somewhere. The commitment was implied. That "yet" was even worse. The conversation I dreaded was a car crash that I could see coming, and I was only making it worse by bracing for it.

I needed to get these two out of my office so I could stuff my existential angst back in a mental cupboard somewhere. It would have to be a different cupboard from the one where I had shoved my attraction to Aaron. That one had a faulty lock, or a false back leading me into another world without my permission. This one would be more secure. It would have to be.

THE DAY BOTH WENT TOO FAST AND DRAGGED. I had meeting after meeting, call after call, but I made time to check my phone between each one and felt the pop of happiness each time there was another text from Aaron. He texted me the most on his lunch break, which didn't line up with mine, but it was an extra little boost to come back to twenty new messages from him. He told me about his day, told me he missed me, detailed his schedule for the week, wondered what I was doing and how I was feeling.

That big black truck was waiting for me at the end of the day, lifting my spirits even higher. Good sex and a personal chauffeur on a dark winter evening was a deal I could not pass up. The interior of the cab hit me with warmth, and Aaron's smile was warmer still when I launched myself over to his side to cover his mouth with mine. He had gone home to change before coming to get me, that lemongrass citrus smell of him fresh from the shower and stronger than ever.

"Hey, beautiful," he said in a low tone, once I had pried myself off of his lips. He smirked, and his eyes sparked, roving over my face. "I like your mouth." He stared at my berry pink lipstick for a long moment, stroking my jaw and bottom lip with his rough thumb. He wasn't wearing gloves, but his hands were warm. His stomach rumbled, loud enough for me to hear, killing the moment.

I laughed. "Should we go make supper?" The ingredients for shepherd's pie were in my fridge waiting for us. It would be our only chance to eat together this week, with evening events starting to fill my calendar the closer we got to the holidays.

He chuckled and let me get settled into my seat before navigating out of the university lot. "I guess my last protein bar was a while ago. I had it in the truck on the way to the Brookside job."

So cold and utilitarian. I was happy to be able to feed him tonight. I wanted to shower him with comfort, with hot food and soft places to stretch out. I wanted to give him a refuge from cold stone and mortar, from chalky protein bars swallowed between jobs.

I shook my head at myself. I wasn't going to get sentimental or nurturing. We were going to have fun, enjoy each other, keep things breezy.

We kept things breezy all through chopping up veggies and browning meat, through the snuggling we did after supper, and the sex that followed. We fell asleep together intertwined, and I woke up to another little note. Still light and breezy.

We kept things light and breezy even as my events schedule filled up over the next few weeks. I got used to that black truck parked at the curb waiting for me, no matter how late my event ran, got used to the notes on my pillow, the texts checking in, and how every day another one of his things appeared and found a spot at my place.

My bathroom shelf now held his toothbrush and deodorant. My shoe rack had a pair of his shoes hanging over the edge. A few shirts and a sweater had found their way into a neatly folded pile on the chair in my bedroom. Protein bars appeared in my cupboard, and a shaker cup and protein powder now had a spot on my counter.

We slipped into a rhythm that lulled me and quieted all my anxieties. Quiet chats over supper, makeouts on the couch, laughing with friends at the pub when my events schedule allowed. I almost never wondered when it would all fall apart.

FRIDAY NIGHT WAS THE MUCH-FRETTED-OVER School of Social Work banquet. I was in my knee-length black dress for the occasion, a cute, high-necked fit and flare, with dark tights and flats, and my gold wrap cardigan to make it more festive. I'd curled my short bob and mussed it into waves.

The event ran smoothly, even with all the student

volunteers I had to wrangle. Dr. Gossman's eagle eye and pursed mouth oversaw all of it with an air of withholding judgment, except when she was on stage or glad-handing donors, charm and wit personified. I admired her ability to command a room, but I would be happy to be done with this particular event.

The takedown afterward took nearly as long as the setup, the volunteers tired and harder to keep on task. I knew Aaron had likely been waiting for nearly an hour by the time I walked out into the lobby to find him. He had been up since five a.m. I felt like I had been on my feet for twenty-four hours straight, and my comfortable flats were starting to rub as my feet swelled.

I spotted Aaron at the very back of the lobby, leaning against a column with one massive shoulder, like Samson testing its strength. Seeing him out in the world, out of my bed, his coat casually slung over one of his crossed arms, his biceps straining at his color-blocked sweater, the drapey knit loving his form, was overwhelming. He had waited for me. He was still waiting for me.

I started over to him, but Dr. Gossman caught me before I could make my escape.

She looked as fresh as ever, not a hair of her smooth chignon out of place, lipstick perfect, a large, sleek bag hooked over her forearm. If I hadn't seen her do it, I would not have believed she had spent a whole night making speeches and individually greeting every table of donors. She launched directly into debriefing and her plans for building the event up even bigger for next year. Her ambition and energy were impressive, but I was longing for bed.

It was a full twenty minutes before I could extricate myself with assurances that I'd send her my full debrief and a report on ways to scale up for the future.

I looked over at Aaron. He had parked himself in my sightline and was leaning against another post, phone in hand, shoulders slumping with fatigue.

He gave me a tired half-smile when I walked over. "Ready to go?" His voice was a gruff rumble that tugged at me.

"In a minute," I said. Stepping into the warmth of his chest, I put my arms around him and hugged him, putting all the gratitude and care I could into the press of our bodies together. His arms folded around me and his beard caught my hair as he rested his cheek briefly on me. I wanted to sink into him.

The rumble in his chest resolved into words. He was talking, and I had been too tired to notice. I tuned in to hear him say, "...so I'll drop you off and head to the farm. I'm hoping to finish up in time to spend Sunday with you, but we'll see how it turns out."

"Wait, why are you going to the farm?"

"Rob texted. One of their retaining walls crumbled. I'm going to head to my parents' place tonight so my dad and I can start working on it first thing tomorrow."

"Who's Rob?" I was too fuzzy with exhaustion for this conversation.

"Alice's husband." I must have looked blank because he shook his head and took my arm, towing me gently out toward the coats. "Alice, my sister. Rob, her husband. They have a dairy farm. I'm heading out to help them."

I nodded as he helped me into my coat. I understood that he wasn't coming home with me, and that was all I needed to know. His truck was waiting for us at the curb, on and heating.

The drive home was drowsy. Aaron spoke, but I couldn't string together a response. Lights blurred and flickered through my half-closed eyes. I felt the cold air blowing on me and realized my door was open. We had stopped, and Aaron had had time to come around to my side before I'd come to.

"There's no parking, again." He was frustrated. "Do you need me to come up with you, or will you make it? I don't want to leave the truck blocking the street."

I gathered my things. "I'll be okay." The cold had helped me snap out of my stupor.

He helped me slide down and walked me to the sidewalk.

"Thanks for waiting for me." I could see headlights turning up the end of the street in the distance. "I'll be fine. Text me when you get there safe."

He leaned in for a sweet, cold kiss. I kissed him back briefly but pushed him away almost immediately. "There's a car coming."

"Goodnight, Ev."

I knew he would wait at the curb until I got in, so I hurried as best I could, fumbling through my bag for my keys with hands numb from cold and exhaustion.

I had to figure out what I was going to do with him. I got inside and leaned back against the door.

One thing I knew for sure: I already missed him.

Chapter Seventeen

❧

I had a lonely weekend without Aaron. He kept me updated sporadically with pictures and texts, working too hard to stop very often. One picture he sent had his dad in the background, a barrel-chested older man who looked like he could break rocks with his fists. Aaron had his nose and hair color. I smiled as I closed our text thread. I needed to do it before I started wearing his sweater and drinking his protein shakes.

Thankfully, Lucy was free to get a coffee at my neighborhood cafe. I had to get out of my empty little place for a few hours. The cafe a few streets over was cheerfully garish, painted in yellow and green. Bookshelves stuffed with second-hand books lined two walls. We got settled with our drinks and listened to the barista work while we looked out of the big picture window that took up the whole front of the cafe. The rhythm of making coffee provided a soothing sound landscape—the buzz of the grinder, the hiss of the steamer, the chatter of eager customers, and neighbors greeting each other across the room.

Looking at house listings was another distraction, even if it still surprised me that my friends were all doing this now. Grace had just told me she was looking at condo listings too. Soon enough, everyone in this group would be a property owner. Meanwhile, I'd been hesitant to get house plants because I didn't want them to die when I moved.

As she opened another listing for us to look at, she glanced at me sideways. "You and Aaron are settling in well together. Hearing you at the pub the other night sounded like he's pretty much moved in."

"Oh no. I mean, he's got a few things at my place, but we're still keeping things casual."

"Casual." She cocked her head, birdlike. "That's what you call casual? His stuff at your place, and being together every day for a month?"

"He's at the farm right now."

"The exception that proves the rule."

I shrugged uncomfortably. "I mean, you guys dated. It's not serious. Just hanging out and enjoying having someone around."

She snorted. "Honey, we did not *date*. We had one date and one awkward kiss and then agreed to be friends. That's not at all what's going with you. And I've seen Aaron do casual dating since then. This is not casual Aaron. This is Aaron who's probably been telling his nonna that you'd make cute grandbabies together."

"No." It came out before I could close my mouth. I pressed my lips together to seal in the rest of my bubbling thoughts. The black hole was back, edging up in my periphery. I wanted to banish it, but I didn't know how. For Lucy, the idea of making plans, putting down deep roots, letting someone in, building something together, was natural, normal. I still couldn't verbalize the end date I saw looming, for whatever I had with Aaron, for the life I had now.

Lucy was still staring at me with concern. But she misread my reaction. "Oh, I mean I didn't mean he was literally talking about having kids. It was just a figure of speech. I'm sorry to freak you out!" She turned thoughtful. "None of our group has really talked about kids at all, apart from how cute baby Rosie is. I don't think you need to worry about it."

I shook my head. "It's not something that's come up. You just caught me off guard, that's all."

Lucy seemed ready to accept that and turned back to her listings and her latte.

I shrugged off all my insecurities and focused on the house hunt with her. "What about that two-bedroom on Ashburn? Did it have a finished basement?"

She pulled it up again, and we discussed its pros and cons and whether the bathroom needed remodeling. I summoned up all the enthusiasm Lucy needed, and she marked which ones she was going to follow up with her realtor about.

She walked me home, still debating what percentage she should put down and whether she should increase her upper range to cast a wider net. I nodded and commiserated in the right places, half-listening, still stuck on grandbabies and nonnas.

THE NEXT FEW DAYS I WENT THROUGH THE motions, checking my lists, crossing things off, putting my bright events smile on when needed, sneaking peeks at my phone like an addict. I zoned out of regular life and focused only on my next contact with Aaron.

Wednesday evening finally arrived, and with it, a big black truck pulled up right in front of the admin building. Waltzing over to it, I popped into the cab with an energetic heave. Aaron was waiting for me, torso turned toward me, beaming at me like we'd been apart for months. I launched myself across the wide seat and into his arms for a hug, crushed against his jacket, my legs twisted behind me. I didn't care how awkward it was. It was glorious to breathe him in again.

He smelled like cold air and bonfire and citrus. He pulled back enough to look me in the eye and smile again, and then swooped in for a quick, hard kiss that had me squirming.

He released me. "Buckle up. We'll finish this later." He sounded as eager as I felt, and I was gratified.

He had picked up pizza for supper, and it was in the back of the cab, filling our space with the smell of yeast and meat.

"So, how was the Biology mixer yesterday? You said everything went well?"

We had texted briefly about it, but I hadn't gone into detail. "It was fine, but I guess Microbiology and Zoology are on the outs and fighting over who will get new lab space? Anyway, it was frosty, even for a winter celebration. Whenever I saw the two deans get into some sneering conversation, I would interrupt and ask one of them a question. I kept having to look up appropriate biology icebreakers. I eventually ran out of 'what's your favorite microorganism and why,' and just asked Dr. Baumler if he had any pets."

Aaron chuckled, "Smart. Everyone likes talking about pets, right?"

"Yeah, that's what I thought. But it turns out his cat recently died. So it was a bit dicier than I thought it would be."

"Oh no."

"Yup, all that punch got the emotions flowing. He showed me a bunch of pictures with tears in his eyes. It was a really sweet cat. I almost cried too, but I think it was the lack of sleep getting to me."

"Not sleeping? You having trouble again?" He shot a quick look of concern my way.

"A little. It's not a big deal. Sometimes my mind races at night and all my relaxation tricks don't help." I lightened my tone. "But I always fall asleep eventually. I just haven't had anyone around to sex me into slumber."

I caught a glimpse of his smile as he turned his head to check his mirrors before changing lanes and making the turns onto my street. The parking gods favored us for once, and we nabbed a spot a few doors down.

Aaron took my gloved hand as we crossed the street, only dropping it when we got to my door. I struggled with the lock on the door as I did almost every day, the old lock sticky and prone to moisture getting in and freezing it shut. After a few failed attempts, Aaron sighed deeply. I looked up, still jamming the key at the lock.

"Why do you never ask for help?" His tone was exasperated.

I lifted a shoulder defiantly. "Why would I? It always works eventually." The moment jabbed a pin at our little bubble of happiness, my irritation helping me chip away the last of the ice and get my key in.

"I could bring some de-icer, or you could talk to the landlady. I still say she should install a proper deadbolt. I could install it myself if you want."

I finally turned the key in the lock. "See, it works. I'll talk to her when I get to it. You don't need to buy me anything."

He huffed but thankfully left it at that. We stepped inside, and I went to change while he served us pizza and poured us wine, falling back into an easy rhythm again. When I walked back in, he was lounging back with his feet up in what had become his spot on the couch. He had a plate of pizza in hand. His hoodie wrapped loosely around his torso, and his worn jeans looked as soft as cashmere.

I felt a pinch in my chest, thinking that if he'd been in my bed, I would have been sleeping just fine. His warmth and his snuggly bear hugs would have lulled me faster than any meditation app. I shook it off. I had been sleeping by myself for the past thirty years, and I wasn't about to forget how to do it. I was just having a temporary glitch.

I grabbed the remote for the TV and put it on my current favorite background fireplace, one with just crackling logs and no music. He grinned at my choice. As a former country boy, he was used to real fires.

"Pizza looks good," I said. "What did you get?"

"Well, after you said you didn't care, I did my usual. Sausage, olives, pepperoni, and hot peppers."

I took my first bite. It was cool enough to eat quickly, but I savored it. Pizza really was that magical food that was good at any temperature.

We sipped our wine and chatted about the day as we ate, on opposite sides of the couch. I tucked one foot under his thigh to keep my toes warm and propped the other foot up on top of his leg. He rubbed at it absently as he drank his wine, telling me about a job where getting progress pay was like pulling teeth and another where the owner insisted on following him around like he was going to deface his basement if he wasn't closely watched.

"He should just install a nanny cam and be done with it. There's hardly anything down there anyway, and most of it is covered up with plastic so it doesn't get dirty. I think he thinks we'll pee down the basement drain."

"Is that a thing people do?"

"Sure, if you're desperate and there's no bathroom, you could. I haven't had to yet. I just take a quick break if I need to."

"That's not very pleasant, to have to wait and time your bathroom breaks."

He shrugged. "It's all part of it. It's not a big deal. I would never ask to use Mr. Paranoid's bathroom. He'd probably follow me in." He smiled at the look on my face. "We'll be out of his hair after tomorrow anyway so he can go back to whatever he does. I suspect spying on his neighbors." He pushed his thumb into the arch of my foot until I stretched it and sighed.

"What other weird clients have you had?"

"So many. It's just part of working for people. People are unique."

"You can say that again. I guess both of us have to deal with all kinds of personalities."

"I think you get that more than I do. I do most of my communication by email. I don't usually have to deal with them as much on the job. Very few people want to be around when we're working."

"Have you ever turned down a job because of a client?"

"Yeah, there have been a few times. Once I remember I got a really weird vibe from this couple. I swear there was a body in the wall that they wanted me to brick over. They were being so shifty about it."

My eyes widened. "What did you do?"

"I told them I was booked and that I couldn't get to their job after all. I kept an eye on the news though, just in case there was an unexplained disappearance."

"You didn't want to report that?"

"What, that I went to a basement and the owners were odd? There are a lot of odd people in the world."

I supposed there were odd people everywhere. But Elmdale was like a small town sometimes, with a cast of characters that had to be seen to be believed. "True. Sometimes people are just awkward. It doesn't mean they've murdered someone and are trying to get you to hide the evidence."

"Right, exactly." He patted my foot and reached for the other. I swapped them gratefully, and we sat for a bit in comfortable silence, my toes curling as he got to a particularly tender spot.

We watched the man's hand come into frame to adjust the logs and throw a new one on. He was wearing a plaid shirt for peak authenticity. The fire popped merrily. "I love it when the hand comes in," I said, pointing with my wine glass.

"Yes, it makes for riveting cinema," Aaron teased. I nudged his side with my foot in retribution, aiming for ribs. He twisted and grabbed my foot, laughing. He settled it down on his leg again firmly, and I relented.

"If you want to see a roaring fire in person, you should come to my parents' place with me sometime. We usually have a fire inside in the evening, and sometimes a big bonfire outside if it's not too cold."

"Oh? Will I get to see you chopping wood to show off?" I teased.

"Well, I certainly won't deny you if you beg." His voice got gravelly as he teased me back, and I knew exactly what he was picturing.

"Beg? On my knees?" I pursed my lips coyly, considering.

"You do great work on your knees, in my experience" was his drawling reply.

I squeezed my thighs together and squirmed. If I slid my foot over his lap would I find him hard?

Evidently, he wasn't as worked up as I was, because he patted my foot and returned to our earlier conversation. "If you came to the farm, I could teach you how to chop wood." He continued in a rush, visibly excited at the idea of me coming with him.

"There's tons to do there in the winter. We could take out the snowmobiles even. Though if we did that, my nephews would definitely tag along. Literally. They sit in a tube tied to the back, and I tow them. They rarely let me go out alone if I'm heading out."

"Wow, that does sound like fun." My smile felt stiff and frozen on my face, but Aaron didn't seem to notice.

"Yeah, you'd love it. We could spend the day, and we could even visit my sister on her farm. Introduce you to the ladies."

"The ladies?" Why was I suddenly picturing an old-timey brothel? Would I make my curtsies to the head madam?

"The cows. They're all ladies, obviously. Though some are not very well-mannered."

"If someone was milking me, I doubt I'd be all that polite." Maybe I would switch to nut milk for this week's grocery shop.

"You make a good point. So, when should we plan our epic adventure to farm life? We can show up anytime. You could come with me this Sunday if you don't have an event."

I was deeply uncomfortable, but Aaron kept nibbling the chocolate I'd brought out for dessert and watching the fake fire, oblivious. My feet had drawn back near me so I was rolled up into a ball. I shrugged my throw blanket tighter around my shoulders and draped it over my feet, cocooned. If I could have built myself a whole blanket fort, I might have.

Everything that I'd been ignoring in the name of "light and breezy" started bubbling back up with a vengeance. I couldn't get away from it. The protein shaker on the table suddenly looked ominous. The thought of his soap in my bathroom brought a burn in the back of my throat. His shirt on my bedroom chair tightened my chest. What had I been doing, thinking I could just have no-strings fun with him? The strings were everywhere.

He continued, totally unaware. "My sister would be thrilled to meet you. She's been bugging me for a while to bring you to Sunday lunch."

He'd been talking to his family about me. How long was "a while"? Lucy had been right about all of it. I struggled for nonchalance. "I don't think it'll work for me." I could be vague about time if he could. "My work schedule is pretty packed with weekend events for the next few weeks." There. That was breezy enough.

"You'll be all done in two weeks, right?"

Dammit. He had my schedule memorized. "Oh, right. I forgot the date. Well, I'll check my calendar and get back to you. I don't remember it off the top of my head."

He looked at me now fully, finally assessing my withdrawn posture. I could see the wheels in his head turning, putting it together.

"Evelyn," he said, with what I thought might be irritation. "You don't have to come if you don't want to. I just thought you'd like to see where I grew up, meet my family."

He hesitated and then spoke again, a little slower. "I'd also thought that because you don't have family here, you might want to come join us for Christmas."

He sounded like he was easing his way through a glassware store, not sure what he was going to knock over. He didn't realize that if he broke something, I wouldn't make him buy it.

"I guess I thought that if you were coming for Christmas, it might be more fun for you if you knew everyone already." Another long pause. "That's all." He shifted his shoulders uneasily, reached out a hand as though he wanted to pull me toward him, and stopped. I had managed to make him as uncomfortable as I felt.

He had been doing a lot of thinking where I was concerned. He'd blown right past thinking to planning. I didn't have the words to tell him about feeling pressed up against the glass of his normal family life. But I felt like he deserved my best effort.

"I'm not really used to big families," I began. He

shook his head, ready to jump in with a rebuttal, but I held up my hand. "And I don't need you to come to my rescue. I'm used to celebrating the holidays by myself. I have my traditions. I'll video-chat with my aunt. I'll volunteer for a shelter on Christmas Day, help them serve a meal. I have things I do." I didn't want his pity invite either, but I didn't know how to say it without sounding bitter.

"I wasn't coming to rescue you, and I'd hardly call seven people a big family," he started, but checked himself when he saw my expression. "Okay, so maybe you and I can make a new tradition together. Boxing Day or something. You don't have to see my family for Christmas. What about the week after? Or for New Year's? We can set off fireworks at the farm."

"You're not getting it." The words were starting to come, tumbling past the freeze I'd been under. If I didn't speak now, he'd keep coming up with perfectly reasonable solutions to any obstacle I put in our path. His decisions had all been made, his path decided. "You can't help yourself. You need to have an answer, a fix, a solution, for everyone."

I couldn't sit still any longer. I pushed up, extricating myself from my blanket, and picked up our glasses and the leftover chocolate. He started to help, but I shook my head and he stopped. I stayed in the kitchen for a few minutes, rinsing glasses, trying to marshal my thoughts, sick to my stomach.

I came back and stood in the doorway. Aaron looked at me, worried now. I hated to see so much concern on his face, his brow wrinkled with a deep crease. All his feelings were at the surface, catching me up in the whirlpool of his emotions, spinning me around and making it impossible to think. I tried taking in a breath. Breathing was important. In. And out. It had to come out after.

I sat down in the armchair across from the couch, needing an extra few feet of distance. I cleared my throat. Aaron waited, visibly patient, holding himself in check. Was he planning his negotiation tactics? Preparing his counteroffer? I wasn't sure what he had in mind, but I knew that I couldn't have any part of it.

"Aaron," I started, but didn't have anything to follow it up. I tried again. "Aaron." Still nothing.

"I'm listening," was all he said, too calmly.

What was I going to say? "I want to have a Define the Relationship talk," I said, more firmly than I felt. "I mean, I don't want to, but I think we should." I trailed off, uncertain.

"Okay." He was leaning forward, elbows on knees, brows drawn, focusing on me intently. I had the feeling that he would be able to recite the whole conversation word for word. Yet to me, the whole thing was a blur of confused feelings and half-formed thoughts.

"I like you." I felt like I was in high school. "But I'm not looking for a relationship right now." That was something people said, right? "And I'm not your project to save or help or look after. I don't need anything from you." I sat back, indicating that it was his turn to speak with a hand wave. I was trembling all over. My teeth were chattering so I clenched my jaw until they stopped.

"Evie. *Like* doesn't describe how I feel about you. I can't pretend I haven't fallen for you." He put his head in his hands for a moment, pulling on his hair in frustration. His hands rubbed down his face. "I'm not sure what you think a relationship is, but from where I sit, we're already in one. This is what you call a relationship."

His hands were clasped now, elbows on knees again. He looked like he was praying, or maybe pleading. "I don't know if you and I have the same idea of what a relationship means. That's the problem I'm running up against right now."

So he wasn't going to address the other thing at all? Wait, fallen for me? Absolutely not going there. "I know what relationships are. You don't need to condescend to me just because I didn't have a dad." I was suddenly furious.

"Wait, wait. I'm not saying that you don't." Those hands reached out toward me now, definitely pleading. "I just don't know if our pictures are the same, that's all. How many healthy adult relationships have you witnessed up close?" I could tell he was trying to say it carefully, once again easing through the glass display shelves, but he didn't know he'd knocked a gravy boat with his elbow, shattering it behind him as he went.

"I'm not going to answer that. I don't need to explain anything to you." Hurt was manifesting as scorn now, my words dripping with it. I had a vicious urge to twist a knife in a place I thought would bleed. "I think there are probably other people who need you, if you really need a project to take on. Why don't you run off and interfere in their lives, and leave me out of it?" My teeth were chattering freely now, the stress in my body needing to come out somewhere.

"Ev," he tried again, still trying for reasonable, but his voice had a definite edge now. Was he angry with me? I couldn't stand to have this talk any longer. He had to go. I raised again my hand to stop him.

"Aaron, please go. I can't do this." He looked like he wanted to keep going with this, like there could be an endpoint where we wound up on the same side. I shook my head.

"Please." I was embarrassed that my voice wavered even on that one short word, the unshed tears evident to both of us. I couldn't speak anymore, or I would cry.

He didn't want to leave. He wanted to hash it out. He wanted forever. I could see it all over him, even though he was getting a little blurry around the edges. He got up, slowly.

"Okay. Okay. I'll give you some space," he said tightly. I could hear the "but" ringing unsaid at the end of the sentence. I knew he'd want to circle back to this conversation again. I hoped it wouldn't be anytime soon.

He stood at the doorway to the kitchen for a while, just looking at me. I couldn't look back. I didn't want to see anything about myself in his face. Eventually, he saw himself out, and I sat there shivering, burning off adrenaline, frozen in place. After a while, I got up and burrowed into bed, not capable of even splashing water on my face. I lay awake for most of the night. When sleep eventually came, it was an interrupted doze, and I felt even less rested when I woke.

Chapter Eighteen

❦

I had dark circles under my eyes. I'd realized that concealer wasn't going to do much for them, so I had skipped it. It was too much effort. I had no in-person meetings, but I did have an event I was hosting later. I threw my makeup bag into my backpack. I would put some on in the afternoon when I was feeling up to it. I considered calling a cab but decided that the walk would probably do me good, and at least wake me up before work.

The weather didn't register at all. It could have been sunny or cloudy or snowing, but I didn't notice. My eyes were blurry the whole walk, the wind in my face bringing tears rolling down my cheeks and disappearing into my scarf, leaving a frosty trail behind. I walked completely by rote, neither slow nor fast, checking for traffic automatically as I crossed the streets, letting my feet take me along.

My mind was blank. I didn't once think of Aaron's eyes so concerned and sad on mine, or the way he had held his hands out to me, begging me to let him in. I didn't think of how cozy he was, how comfortable we were together, how he seemed to understand me, how easy it was to talk to him, how hot he made me. I didn't think of any of it. I didn't think of how presumptive he was, or how he thought he could fix everyone's life, how he always knew best, how he craved being needed.

Melanie gasped when she saw me. It was understandable. I had never come to work without makeup, with my hair closer to bedhead than artfully mussed, in an ugly old sweater from back when plus-sized office-appropriate clothing meant tents a stylish grandmother wouldn't wear. I went to my office to strip off my outer layers and change from my boots to indoor shoes.

By the time I made it to the coffee maker, Grace was waiting for me. Damn our efficient and observant admin.

She took me in while she handed me a freshly poured cup, steaming hot. I blew on it to avoid meeting her eyes.

"Do you want to talk about it?" Her voice was so

soft. My eyes prickled, and I blinked furiously. I shook my head. I couldn't talk about it. I actually couldn't speak at all. I had a lump in my throat right around the area of my voice box. I tried clearing my throat, but it didn't budge. I would get that looked at.

"Okay, honey. It's okay. I'll be here if you want to tell somebody. And if you don't want to tell me, that's okay too. But you should talk to someone. It always helps, even if it's hard. Believe me, I know." She rubbed my upper arm up and down twice, brisk and comforting, seeming to sense that I would not be able to handle a hug. She let me escape into my office, and I closed my door, blowing my nose furiously and dabbing eyes that were still watery from my walk.

Just before lunch, after a brief knock, Joel came into my office. My computer had been misbehaving all morning—the screen was out of focus, the lighting was too bright, and it hurt my eyes. I clicked through all my settings, but everything looked normal. It was the most productive thing I'd done all day. Each email took me half an hour or more to compose a response to, no matter how simple the question. I was not even halfway through my unread emails.

I swiveled gratefully to Joel, happy for a distraction even if I was dreading an interrogation.

"Evie, it's time for you to go home," he began, completely no-nonsense. I stared at him in blank confusion. "I got an email from you earlier that was unintelligible, and even if it had made sense, it was meant for Melanie. You're not doing your best work, and everyone here knows it. Take a personal day and head home. The work will still be here after you're feeling better. We can cover for you until then."

"I can't. I have an event at four."

"We've arranged it all. Melanie is going to take my meeting at three-thirty, and I'll head over to host for you. I read up on the event file, and it's all straight-forward. I've already emailed Tanya from Psychology and told her you're sick and heading home. She's expecting me."

I started to protest, but he kept rolling right over me, talking a little louder. "Douglas is on his way to pick you up—he's taking his lunch early so he can drop you at home. We're going to forward your emails and calls to Melanie, and she'll handle anything urgent that comes in. Go put your boots on and get your coat, and I'll forward your emails for you."

He was already behind my chair, giving it a little jiggle to get me to move. He sat down as soon as I got up and swiveled toward my computer, navigating his way through my email settings.

"Take the day tomorrow too. You can do a few things from home to get ready for the event on Saturday, but you don't need to come in." He spun toward my phone and picked up the receiver to start forwarding my calls.

He paused. "Are you still standing there? Get a move on. Douglas will be here soon." He went back to ignoring me, listening to the prompts the phone system gave.

I snapped out of my daze and started gathering my things, putting my shoes back on the mat I had for them, and getting my boots. Joel shut down my laptop, disconnected it from the port, and handed it to me to put in my bag. He ushered me out of my office, taking my arm like he was helping an elderly person across the street.

He walked me to the coat rack, and then outside where Douglas was waiting in his sensible blue sedan. He shut me into the car, walked around to give Douglas a kiss through the open window, and then dashed back in, obviously chilly in his nice black sweater and collared shirt. He hadn't bothered putting a jacket on.

I had never been in the front seat of Douglas's car before, usually letting the lovebirds sit up front together. It was warm from his drive over.

"Let's get you home, my dear," was all Douglas said. He let the radio fill the silence. It was all news at the top of the hour, and I tuned it out.

I thanked Douglas when he pulled up in front of my place. He leaned over and kissed my cheek and told me to call if I needed anything.

As I let myself into my apartment, it occurred to me that they all seemed to know what was going on, even though I hadn't explained anything. Aaron must have told them all about it.

I hated thinking about what he probably said, about what an unreasonable bitch I must look like to all my friends. I couldn't bring myself to check the group chat. Would they have already started a new one without me?

I left my bag right there in the entryway and went straight to my room, stripping down, falling into bed. My eyes kept leaking, and my pillow was damp, but I fell asleep regardless.

I didn't wake up until after six. I felt so groggy, my eyes full of sand and grit, that I went straight to the shower and stood under the steaming hot spray, moving slowly, letting my fatigue swirl down the drain.

I felt more human than I had all day, and even felt like moisturizing. I let it absorb, walking around naked for a few minutes in just my socks before I put my loungewear on. Mum had always said I was a resilient woman born of resilient women. It was true that not much knocked me down for long. I always picked myself back up, packed away what I needed to, and moved on. I could feel some bruised spots on my soul, but they only really hurt if I pressed directly on them.

I picked up my backpack and chucked my now-gross ham sandwich. I made myself some peanut butter toast and chamomile tea, breathing through the sharp pang when I remembered that Aaron had bought it for me. I settled on the couch in the spot that was mine again and put my feet up.

With an action movie on in the background, I finally picked up my phone and turned it back on. I had turned it off before I started work, and now I wasn't sure whether I hoped to find Aaron's name when I turned it on again or not. My phone buzzed nonstop as all the messages came in at once. I turned it face down and let it buzz beside me until it was done receiving. I turned it over. Messages from Grace, Lucy, Joel, and Aunt Bea. Aaron's name was right there. I pressed his name first.

I miss you.

That was it. No demands, nothing further. I moved on to my friends. They had all sent a variant of "thinking of you," "love you," "let me know if you need anything." I sent back hearts.

I opened Aunt Bea's messages next.

We're still on for tomorrow? 5:30 your time ok? I have a date after so I can only chat till 6. #talkingtomynieceismyfave 🌙

Aunt Bea of course didn't know what was going on with me this week. I wished I could go back in time to the last time we'd talked, back when Aaron and I were still full of possibility, just a fun romantic fling to sigh over.

I let her know I'd be there. I didn't know what to say to Aaron. I didn't want to hurt him any more than I already had, and I didn't want to be hurt anymore either. Perhaps a clean break was best, even if it felt like everything was hanging unresolved. No, what more was there to resolve? We didn't want the same things at all. It was for the best to leave it.

I fell asleep on the couch with comforting fake explosions in the background, woke up late, and transferred to my bed. Maybe I would just sleep for the rest of my life instead of dealing with anything. It was the perfect plan. I was a genius.

It didn't seem possible that there could be sleep left within me, but the next day I was still in bed at noon. I had to drag myself up and get coffee going. Work was still waiting for me.

Grace and Joel had both sent me emails summing

up all of the work they had taken care of. Thanks to them and Melanie, there were no major problems for me to deal with. I would feel very dispensable if I didn't know what an effort it had been to do their jobs and mine and how much they'd had to rearrange to help me.

I no longer felt embarrassed by what Aaron would have told them, or at least not very embarrassed. I wasn't ready to call Grace and ask her about it, but it was evident that they didn't think less of me. The group chat had started up again, innocuous and playful, talking about upcoming concerts and who was in to buy tickets. Only Aaron had been quiet on there. My heart panged at the effort they were making, how they were going out of their way to show me I was still included, still welcome. It gave me hope, that maybe there could be a day where I could hang out with them all again like nothing had ever happened. Almost as if I hadn't blown up my easy friend group by getting in too deep with Aaron. Like the past month or two had been a trail of footprints I could wipe away or cover the mess I'd made with a fresh layer of snow.

Work still waited, a welcome distraction from my thoughts. There were emails to answer, shared spreadsheets to update, and check-in calls to make. It took me all of three hours to get my tasks done for the day, and I closed my work files with even more gratitude for my coworkers.

I took my time making supper and settled in with my plate of pasta and my laptop stacked on a few books on my coffee table, logging on to our video call right at five-thirty. Aunt Bea was already there waiting for me, her phone held below chin height at an angle that would win her no social media likes. She had her bifocals on and was looking down at me through the bottom half, the chain for her glasses swinging next to her neck. Her close-cropped grey hair was jazzed up with a streak of pink in the front. The skin under her chin was starting to sag, and the lines around her eyes and mouth were getting deeper. She was beautiful. I missed her so much. The lump in my throat returned, larger than before. Maybe I had a tumor.

"My terror!" she squealed when she saw me. She'd been calling me some permutation of "evil" ever since we moved east to live with her. The kids at my new school had teased me and called me "Evil-in" for months. When she found out, she wanted to help take the sting out of it. Now instead of "treasure," I got "terror," and instead of 'darling' I got "darnling."

I croaked out a "hi" around the block in my larynx. I saw her pause and take me in.

"Evie? What's wrong, my beastly?" She tilted her

phone closer to her face to inspect me. I was now getting a view almost straight up her nose. I started laughing, and all of a sudden I was crying big heaving sobs, snot bubbling. I set my plate down untouched, buried my head in my arms, and wept, with my aunt thousands of miles away from me and right in front of me. The ache of missing her was a physical pain, my chest burning.

I cried for what felt like hours, shaking with it, until I calmed enough to hear Aunt Bea singing my favorite childhood song, "You Are My Sunshine." That made me smile, the subtle snark of her choice, and it helped me taper off into hiccups. The song had been my favorite right up until I realized how sad it was and then refused to sing it anymore. But Aunt Bea had always been perverse and kept singing it to me even after I told her it was not a happy, pretty song. She had only smiled maddeningly and said every song had its place and sad things could be pretty too.

Mum had been too practical to interfere with our little squabbles, and too tired, too busy taking care of me and her ailing mother, and then later, too sick herself. I missed her. I wished I could have known her before life had beaten her down into grim stoicism. I choked on that thought. Maybe she would have been the same, maybe it was bred in the bone.

Granny had lived with a pretty harsh view of the world too.

Aunt Bea had always been different from the other Stone women. Lighter, more playful, even when life was hard. I often thought of her as a literal bee, flitting from flower to flower, not caring if her butt got covered in pollen, making something sweet with whatever she found. She was so fully herself.

"I miss you. And I miss Mum," was all I managed to say without breaking down again.

"Evie, I miss you too. And I miss Dot, and I miss my mum." Dot was too whimsical a name for my mother, but that's what Aunt Bea had always called her. Dorothy was for everyone else, only Aunt Bea got to use Dot. She kept humming, waiting for me to be ready to talk.

"Am I keeping you from your date?" I checked the time. It was only five forty-seven. I could have sworn I'd cried for centuries. I felt wrung out.

"Darnling, they will wait. Don't you worry. I'm worth the wait." She preened a little to make me laugh.

"You certainly are, Aunt Bea."

"Now, it's time to pick up your plate and take a bite. Then tell Auntie all about it." She fixed me with her bifocaled glare until I obediently picked up my plate. She let me chew and swallow and take a sip of wine before she told me to "just get on with it."

"I don't know how to talk about it." I waved my fork at her helplessly. She raised her eyebrows, like "so?"

"Okay, okay. So there's a few things. There's Aaron. He's picturing some big future with me. He wants to introduce me to his family. Take me to their farm. Spend Christmas with them." I stopped there. I couldn't talk about him anymore. "Then there's being with this group of friends. They're all so sure of what they're doing in life—buying houses, settling down, making big plans for the future. I don't have any future that I can see. I just don't stack up when I look at me and I look at everyone around me. I barely made it through high school."

Aunt Bea looked stricken. "Evelyn Louise Stone. Why on earth do you think you don't have a future?"

I couldn't verbalize my black hole. I had only recently become aware it existed. I shook my head and shrugged my shoulders.

"Schooling doesn't give you any more or less of a future. And you know the only reason that you struggled to finish high school is because Dot was so sick and we had to take care of her and work so hard. They were difficult years for both of us. I'm incredibly proud that you managed to finish in spite of everything. Dot was proud of you too. She cried when you came home after your ceremony with your cap and gown still on and your diploma in hand. And Lord knows that woman's tears were as rare as hens' teeth."

My own tears started up again, rolling silently, the dam now smashed open from wherever I'd been storing them for ten years. Mum had been proud of me, I knew that. Aunt Bea had taken time off work to come to the ceremony to take pictures so Mum could see them after.

Aunt Bea continued, more gently, "You're building your future right now. You've already built yourself a good life. You have enough food and a safe place to live. You and I don't ever take that for granted. You have a good, challenging job. You have good friends. You'll keep building on that. What more could any of us ask for a present or a future?"

"I don't know, Aunt Bea." I struggled to find more words. "I just—" I paused. "I only have seven more years until I'm as old as Mum was when she died. I feel like I'm just surviving until then."

The silence stretched between us. I had shocked both of us. I'd never thought about it so plainly before. But it was true. Somehow I'd always felt like I was just marking time, checking each day off until I reached the inevitable end.

Aunt Bea's face had gone white. "You and I both tested negative for the gene. Why would you think that?"

It was true. All the Stone women had gone for genetic testing before Granny died. Granny and Mum both had the gene mutation; Aunt Bea and I did not.

"I don't know. I guess I'm just waiting for the other shoe to drop."

"We lived with cancer nonstop from when you were eleven years old, right up to when you were nineteen. It's understandable that you can't believe your life could be without it. But, my love, I want you to try."

"I don't know how."

"I believe in you, even when you can't." She held my gaze before continuing. "I want you to know that I understand the strange tragedy of outliving your parent. I'm older than Mum was when she died. I feel sad for her that she never got to experience more of life, that she had to work so hard to get by. I feel sad that she's not sitting in the rocking chair across from me, knitting hideous sweaters for her grandchild, cursing when they turn out lopsided, and drinking too much whiskey. But I choose to honor her life by living mine as fully as possible."

She stopped there. We were both crying now. It was so strange to cry at each other's faces without being able to hold on to one another. We each got up to find tissues and came back, more settled after a few vigorous nose blows.

"Darnling, I think you should talk to someone about this. Can one of your friends recommend a counselor for you? Or I could ask mine if she would see you over video call. You don't need to see them forever, but it's time to start living, Evie. My greatest wish is for you to be *fearless*."

I could hear the freedom in the word, the doors blown open in front of me, the paths and possibilities. It called to me. My thoughts and feelings were such a tangle. Maybe fear was at the heart of everything. Was I afraid to try with Aaron because I was afraid to lose him? Loss was exhausting. It had worn me down. I didn't know if I could survive another.

I shook my head. I would have to think about it. "I'll tell you one thing Aaron said that made me so mad, Aunt Bea." I sighed, half finding the humor, half still enraged. "He told me I didn't know what healthy relationships looked like. And then I started to worry he was right. I mean, there wasn't a lot of romance around us."

She thought about it a moment. "You know, Evie, I have yet to find a life partner. But I remain open to it. I think true partnership is a gift." She smiled at me. "Dot had you very young, and on her own, so you didn't see much in the way of romance. But you saw us. We were committed to each other and helped each other along the way. Good romantic partnership is much the same. The lust may fade, but trust and friendship is the foundation that remains."

She took a sip of water and continued, smiling sympathetically at the fresh tears slipping down my cheeks, "I think you would be a wonderful life partner. You are loyal to the core, and have so much love to give."

"Thanks, Aunt Bea. For everything."

"I have every confidence you'll figure it out." Her doorbell rang. "Oh, they must have wondered what was taking me so long. I should go get that."

"You go enjoy your date. Thanks for the chat. Love you."

"Love you too, devil-cakes." She blew kisses dramatically and signed off, leaving me smiling through my sniffles. Aunt Bea had always been cagey with details about her love life. When I was younger, I figured she'd probably either been too busy taking care of me and Mum to date, or maybe she was dating but felt guilty about taking time for herself so she kept it quiet. I didn't know why she didn't share more with me now, but we usually kept things light when we talked. We'd both had enough of the heavy for a lifetime.

I checked my phone. No texts from Aaron. I missed him. He was still the most comforting person I could think of to call. I wanted to wrap myself in him even while I told myself all the ways it couldn't possibly work.

Chapter Nineteen

❦

I pulled my life together by sheer force of will for the next weeks. Hosting events, updating spreadsheets, showing up to work looking professional. I researched up cat adoption in my spare time and moved a weighted blanket in and out of my online shopping cart. The protein powder was hidden away in the cupboard under my sink, and the rest of Aaron's things were buried in a pile of linens in my closet. He hadn't texted to ask for them back. One T-shirt did find its way under my pillow, but I wasn't sure how that had happened.

I'd given up on cooking altogether. My diet was toast and peanut butter sandwiches. Cereal for supper. Precut carrot sticks when I felt alarmed at my lack of vitamin intake.

My friends were obviously concerned. Grace had

given me her therapist's name when I asked, and Dr. Munro had squeezed me in. The first meeting had felt like an interview, with her getting all my background, and near the end, my hopes were not high for our chances together. My throat was sore from talking, and I didn't feel any better. I nearly made up my mind not to come back.

But after she had closed her chart and capped her pen, she had looked at me and said, "You've been managing a lot, all on your own. You being here is very brave, and I want to acknowledge that. I'd like to leave you with a thought for the week. Any time you start to worry about the future, I want you to ask yourself, 'What if it all works out? What if the future is better than I could imagine?' That's all you have to do. I just want you to hold on to the *what if* for now."

I decided right then to come back and try again.

I faithfully did my homework for the week. I looked around my apartment and thought, *What if I stayed?* All my shabby, mostly second-hand furniture looked a bit brighter in that light.

At work, Joel and Grace paused whenever I came into the room, making me wonder if I'd been the subject of conversation. I was surprisingly unselfconscious. Instead I smiled at them and thought of how our friendship might deepen and change if I stayed, how we might look back at this time and laugh or sigh at this momentary blip in our friendship. I saw my workload in new ways with too, with thoughts of streamlining and innovating, with ideas for future projects that excited me.

The group chat was still active, and the conversation had shifted to who was going to do open houses with Lucy. Aaron had of course volunteered, and his name on my screen had been a tiny guilty knife prick in my chest. He was quieter than usual but still responded occasionally. I couldn't bring myself to ask Joel directly how he was doing, even though I knew he was spending time with him. I got the impression that Aaron was pretty wrecked. The feeling was mutual.

Other than that, I didn't think about Aaron at all most days, didn't press on that particular bruise. But at night when my brain had nothing else to do, it whirred to life with him. It manufactured moments we never had, mingled in with moments we'd shared.

I pictured him, fixated on me, but not on the me that was standing right in front of him. He was fixated on future me, the one by his side, surrounded by family, opening presents. In that version, he had a tiny ring-sized box waiting in his pocket. His family was enormous—at least fifty people crowd the room, determined to get a look at me. Their eyes were a spotlight that picked out each one of my shortcomings. *What if.*

I pictured him with his face in a stubborn mask, brows drawn down. Through his beard, his jaw clenched. He was ready to meddle in my life, to interfere, to tell me he knew best. Mr. Magistrate, giving his ruling and expecting me to fall in line. He made me crazy. I rolled over and tried to knock him out of my head, banging it hard on the pillow.

I pictured his patience, leaning against a cement pillar, waiting for me to extend a hand to him.

I pictured his arm weighing down my ribs, the deep pressure making me work to take a full breath, his nose rubbing into my hair, his chest vibrating as he spoke.

His flaws were more evident to me the longer we were apart, but so were his strengths, two sides of a coin that I flipped endlessly to see whether it would land heads or tails.

Eventually, I slept.

ON THE TENTH OF DECEMBER, A SURPRISE WAITED when I got home from work. I took one look and burst into tears.

The most perfect mini Christmas tree sat in front

of my door, in a burlap-wrapped pot. It was draped with tiny twinkle lights attached to a battery pack and decorated with tinsel. A cute silver star perched on top. A cardboard tag hung from one of the branches, but I knew who had brought it.

I plucked the card off the branch, tears still streaming. It said: "I'm sorry. You were right. Hope this reminds you of home.—Aaron"

It was short and to the point. It said everything it needed to and more. He'd been listening, even while he'd been barging ahead of me. The evidence was right here, the proof in each delicately spiked branch.

I hauled it in and found the perfect spot for it, the twinkle lights throwing a delicate glow. The scent filled my living room. I'd never had a real tree before. I fussed with it a bit longer, making sure it wasn't in a draft, consulting the internet for how moist the soil should be, perfecting the drape of the tinsel.

I had my now-customary bowl of cereal for supper, staring at my tree the whole time. After I was done, I called up Aaron's messages. His last text sat there unanswered. I started composing a response. I stopped. I started again, then deleted it.

I looked at the picture I had saved, the one he took for me on that sparkling sunlit day, with the light bouncing off the snow and ice all around and back onto his face, illuminating him with mini diamonds. His beard was frosty. He was perfect; the skin around his eyes crinkling as he smiled big at the camera, happy just to be texting me a picture.

My thumbs moved on instinct.

I miss you. Call me?

I sent it before I could think better of it, but then I regretted it immediately. I threw my phone down, and it bounced off the couch and onto the floor. I eased around it and let it lie there like a bug I did not want to disturb, taking my bowl to the kitchen to wash.

I was being a coward. Confrontation could be hard for me, but not being able to confront my own phone was a new low. I marched back to the living room, determined. It was ringing.

A wave of relief and anxiety washed over me. I couldn't process everything I was feeling, as usual, but I shook it off and answered.

"I was hoping you'd text." His voice was tinny and far away, road noises in the background. He was driving.

"Aaron, I..." But he was speaking at the same time, the lag from his car speaker scrambling our voices together. We both paused, the silence stretching. "Sorry. Go ahead." Giving way was automatic and slipped out before I could rein in the impulse.

"No, I'm sorry. Shit. I wanted to apologize in person. You were right." He sounded so frustrated. I could almost see him rubbing his face. "I'm on my way to the farm tonight. I'm almost there and my mom is expecting me, but I'd like to talk to you. I could turn around."

"No, you should see your parents. I was going to apologize to you. For not calling earlier. For avoiding you."

"No, I would avoid me too. You're right. I did too much assuming. I shouldn't have assumed. I should have asked, should have checked in. I was just so happy to be with you, I never thought to see how you were feeling." He paused again, but I just sat there, listening, trying to absorb it all. "Douglas said you had a point about me needing a project. I wasn't trying to fix you, not like that. But sometimes it drove me nuts how little you asked of me—it made me feel like I didn't have anything worthwhile to give you. So maybe I do need to be needed, like you said. I'm sorry."

I could hear the blinker indicator now, and the crunch of tires hitting gravel. I guessed he was almost at his parents' place. We didn't have much time.

"Aaron. I want to see you again. I want to try with

you. I want to find out what if." I wasn't explaining myself well, but he seemed to understand.

"What if? I'd like that. I'd like that very much." His voice cracked, the emotion clear. His faults were as clear to me as ever, and I knew I'd uncover more as time went on, but each one came with a strength on the opposite side of that coin.

"I don't want to make any plans. Those still freak me out a little. I have things to work through. And I can do it on my own, but I'd like you there with me. Because...maybe I've fallen for you too." The coin flipped, and the strengths won.

"I'll check in with you. I won't assume a single thing until we've talked about it. Okay?" Everything was quiet now except for his voice, crystal clear like he was sitting next to me. He had made it to the farm and turned off the truck. I would have to let him go in soon.

"Meet you at the pub tomorrow?" I tried for breezy, but my voice was shaking with anticipation and relief.

"I'll be there. Can I pick you up?" He was learning.

"It's supposed to be mild. I'll walk, and you can drive me home. And if you'd happen to want to stay over, I still have a few of your things here somewhere."

"You didn't incinerate them? Kind of you. I'll meet you there then, beautiful Ev."

"What if? I'd like that. I'd like that very much." His voice cracked, the emotion clean. His limbs were as clean to me as ever, and I knew I'd uncover more as

SNOW DANCED DELICATELY AROUND ME IN THICK, fat flakes, landing crystalline on my mitts and scarf, clumping on my lashes, putting my eye makeup to the test. Each soft brush of snow against my cheek was a cold kiss under the pooling light of the streetlamps.

What if it could be even better than I expected? It was a constant refrain. The lightness in those words made trudging through ankle-deep snow easy, anticipation carrying me along. I was going to see him tonight.

A few steps up to that golden-lit carved pub door, a wave at Julia loading up a tray of drinks by the bar, and a moment to collect myself in the coatroom.

A broad shape filling the door frame before I even finished hanging my coat and shaking the rapidly melting snow out of my hair. Aaron.

He leaned against the jamb, taking me in, those eyes sparking again, that grin coaxing one dimple out.

"Hey." He was trying for casual, I could see, maybe still giving me space, letting me lead.

I couldn't keep the delight off my face if I tried. I threw myself into his arms, my mittens still in one hand. He crushed me to him, laughing. His arms were the best spot in the whole world.

"Ev." He sighed, a deep rumble reverberating pleasantly through me. "I've missed you so much. Let's fight and stay next time. Make-up sex. I've always wanted to have it."

"I'm not sure about you planning our next fight already, but I'll take that deal. We can pretend-fight later tonight if you want." I smirked and pulled away to tuck my mittens into my coat pocket, and he followed me deeper into the room.

"Should we make out in here for a bit? I don't think the others will notice." He stroked my jaw, and though he was joking, I knew he'd gladly haul me up against the wall in a heartbeat if I gave the word.

I reached up and twined my arms around his neck, leaning in close to his mouth. Even in the dim light of the coatroom, his eyes were hard to look at, so bright and full of hope and love.

I ducked my head and tucked it against his shoulder. Some things you just couldn't say while staring into someone's eyes. Even someone that you were maybe falling in love with.

"So, remember how I sort of told Grace I wasn't interested in dating you? Or maybe you didn't hear me."

His laugh rang out and interrupted my train of

thought, scattering all the courage I'd built up. "Sorry to disappoint, but there was no way I could have missed it. I remember every word. I also seem to remember you did a lot of staring for someone who wasn't at all interested."

I wasn't sure I'd ever live that moment down. It still brought heat to my cheeks every time I thought of it. "Well. I'm fully ready to take it back now."

"Phew. You had me worried for a second." Sarcasm dripped from his tone, but he rubbed against the side of my face with his chin, nudging me into lifting my face to his again. "We can head in and you can tell Grace you're interested after all, if you want to make it up to me. I'll stand within earshot again." His lips were a whisper from mine now, tempting me.

"I think she's probably figured it out by now. But I can gladly check you out again," I murmured, sinking into his kiss. Our friends would wait for a few minutes, the future would unfold in time. For now, there was this magical kiss, stretching out this moment, potent with possibility and hope.

Epilogue

❦

December 25, one year later.

I clicked the turn signal on and pulled off the highway onto the gravel road. The big black truck plowed through the high drifts piled at the edge of the highway with ease.

My first driving lessons had been in Douglas's car, after the spring thaw, but it hadn't taken long for me to take on the truck. And after snow fell again, Aaron had made sure I could get out of a skid before taking on winter highway driving. Donuts in parking lots after the first big snow had been the perfect training ground.

Next time I'd probably let him drive to the farm, but I wanted to prove to myself that I could do it in the winter just as well as the summer.

I was used to his family now, introduced to them slowly and gradually over our year of dating until I was comfortable with them, but major holidays were a whole new milestone for us. My counselor had been encouraging when I told her I was ready to try, to take another step.

The driving gloves he'd gotten me as an early Christmas gift were grippy on the steering wheel, but the gravel road was slick and icy under the layer of snow, and I slowed to a crawl, trying to adjust to it. Aaron had no comment from the passenger seat, except to flick the hazard lights on. I nodded, even as I was busy with both hands on the wheel, concentrating. It was common sense to indicate we'd be going slower than the country folk used to icy gravel roads.

Finally, I pulled up in front of the festive farmhouse, decked with brightly colored lights all along the roofline, and an inflatable Santa and reindeer in the front yard. Decorations were strewn everywhere I looked, in a cheerily haphazard fashion. It was gaudy and perfect.

Concentrating on the drive had kept me from being nervous about the gifts piled in the back, about whether his mom would like the shortbread I'd made from Granny's recipe Aunt Bea had sent me, about whether my outfit was too dressy for the occasion. I'd packed a change of clothes just in case. All those nerves came crowding back in as soon as the truck was in park.

Aaron slanted me a look under those drawn brows, assessing. "Have I told you today that I love you?"

"I think surrendering your truck to me was a pretty good indication, but I don't mind hearing it again."

He chuckled. "You know they love you. You know I love you. We're going to have a great time. And if the boys get too rowdy, we'll lock them in the barn."

"I've been promised that I'll be able to witness an epic snowball fight. Maybe I'll give a kiss to the winner."

"Consider it won." He leaned over to claim his prize prematurely, and I pushed him back, laughing. He grinned back. "You ready?"

"Absolutely."

Thank you!

Thanks so much for reading Set in Stone! I'm thrilled to be able to share my debut book with you and can't wait to hear what you think!

If you enjoyed it, please consider helping other readers find it by leaving a review. Thank you!

Sign up for my newsletter to read an exclusive bonus snippet of Aaron's POV of the first time sees Evie at the pub! I'd love to keep in touch!

Acknowledgments

I wrote this book as a settler on Treaty 1 territory. It is the territory of the Anishinaabeg, Cree, Oji-Cree, Dakota, and Dene Peoples, and the homeland of the Métis Nation.

One's first book doesn't come into the world without an incredible amount of support. Sprint buddies, beta readers, encouragers, editors, and writers who made themselves available to talk details about publishing: I feel so grateful for all of you.

Shout out to the group chat for your unwavering support. Love you.

Many thanks to the Polite Society NaNo 2020 writing group and to Ashley T. for being a great moderator. The sprints, mutual support, and encouragement were all so valuable.

Thanks to my editor Sarah of Lopt and Cropt for all the wisdom and guidance.

Thanks to beta readers TJ, Kim, Alexis, Ashley, Blair, Lauren, and Heather. I won't name names on who made me cry with their heartfelt enthusiasm for my book. All of your insight made the book stronger.

Special thanks to Sonya, who I'm going to have to hire, because there isn't enough craft beer in the world to repay you.

Thanks to Abra for the beautiful art for my cover. It's a privilege to work on creative projects with you.

Thanks to the extremely multi-talented Jack Harbon for formatting my print and ebooks.

Thanks to Katee Robert, who answered my emails when she didn't have to, and to the Word-makers for sharing their experience and energy.

Finally, thanks to my partner, who is so biased about me I can't ask him for an opinion on anything, and who always makes space for my dreams and plans. I love you.

About the Author

Lynn Camden is a settler in Treaty 1 territory on the beautiful Canadian prairies. She's always looking for romance that thrills and for the coziest possible reading nooks. She began writing her debut novel to combat pandemic doldrums, and swiftly fell in love with writing. When she's not writing, Lynn can be found baking with her kids, watching bad action movies with her husband, sipping margaritas, or gossiping with friends.

Connect at www.lynncamden.com.

9 781777 757700